I0687455

# Portence

## by

## Gini Rifkin

*Fae Warriors, Book 3*

This is a work of fiction. Names, characters, places, and incidents are either the product of the author's imagination or are used fictitiously, and any resemblance to actual persons living or dead, business establishments, events, or locales, is entirely coincidental.

**Portence**

COPYRIGHT © 2017 by Virginia Rifkin

All rights reserved. No part of this book may be used or reproduced in any manner whatsoever without written permission of the author or The Wild Rose Press, Inc. except in the case of brief quotations embodied in critical articles or reviews.
Contact Information: info@thewildrosepress.com

Cover Art by *Debbie Taylor*

The Wild Rose Press, Inc.
PO Box 708
Adams Basin, NY 14410-0708
Visit us at www.thewildrosepress.com

Publishing History
First Fantasy Rose Edition, 2017
Print ISBN 978-1-5092-1660-4
Digital ISBN 978-1-5092-1661-1

*Fae Warriors, Book 3*
Published in the United States of America

**"What in supersymmetry are you doing here?"**

"I came to warn you."

"About what? I don't need your help."

"You needed my help back then, Portence, and you need it now. Why must you always be so stubborn?

"It's poor strategy to bring up what you did to me in the past," she snapped, ignoring his question.

Mouth pressed into a grimace, she stood her ground, fighting to remain calm. Fighting not to slap his face and then fling herself into his arms. They stood in the moonlight staring at one another, he with those golden eyes, clear and penetrating. His expression hot as molten amber.

His five o'clock shadow had slid closer to eight o'clock, deepening the angles of his beautiful face, adding darkness and danger to the sculpted features so angelic when he so chose.

## Praise for Gini Rifkin

"The characters [in *SOLACE*] are well-written and the plot is seamless."

~*Still Moments Magazine (4 Stars)*

~*~

"I had a feeling *BLISS* was going to be as memorable as *SOLACE* (book 1) and I was correct in my assumption."

~*Super Kam (4.5 Stars)*

~*~

"[*A COWBOY'S FATE* is a] must read."

~*Still Moments Magazine (5 Stars)*

~*~

"*IRON HEART* gives the classic epic adventures a run for their money."

~*Sizzling Hot Books (5 Hearts)*

~*~

"Rifkin's [*LADY GALLANT*] is epic in scope, meticulously researched and finely detailed."

~*Romantic Times Book Reviews*

~*~

"[*VICTORIAN DREAM* was] written with a rich depth of detail. Nicely spiced with an underlying sense of mystery and danger."

~*Night Owl Reviews*

~*~

"[In *THE DRAGON AND THE ROSE*] Rifkin is immensely knowledgeable about the story's time period."

~*Romantic Times Book Reviews*

## Dedications

Dedicated to Cousin Mary Ann,
the best PR person in Illinois.
And to the magic around us, seen and unseen.
~*~
With special thanks to The Wild Rose Press, Inc.
and the amazing Amanda Barnett.

# Author's Note

*In the time of myth and legend, man conquered the Fae, sentencing them to a life underground. But when mankind stopped believing in faeries and magic, the human heart grew smaller, the human soul an infinitesimal shade darker.*

*One group of the banished wee folk languished in the darkness. To save this clan, Mother Nature transported them to another planet. They thrived and grew mighty in appearance and intelligence, as well as in their love and reverence for their mother. In gratitude, all members of the rescued tribe faithfully serve the Multiverse in one way or another, be it art, science, philosophy, peacekeeping—or warfare.*

*Now, at Mother Nature's command, the descendants of the Tuatha de Danann have put aside their remembered grievances and returned to Earth. As members of the Fae Warrior Alpha team, Solace, Bliss, and Portence have sworn to do whatever it takes to save the planet.*

*Reptile invaders, led by a goddess gone bad, or possibly gone mad, face the Guardians of the Multiverse—the human's only hope for survival.*

# Friends and Enemies in the Fae Warrior Adventure

The Sisters of Anu—Solace, Bliss, and Portence
Captain Tanner Jackson—Solace's partner
Nathaniel (Nate) Calhoun—Bliss' partner
Dr. Lance Lawson—Port's current partner
Malachi—Fae/sorcerer crossbreed, Port's previous partner
Alfonso—Nate's compadre at the ranch.
Noodge—the Fae sisters' loyal Rapran companion
Mother Nature—aka Mother, aka MoNat
Mercury—Mother's special friend.
Xandora—leader of the Reptiles
Botu—Reptile commander
Thurax—alien mercenary. Portence and Malachi's nemesis
Gorlock—a would-be wizard from the dark side
Hover Rats—more mercenary aliens
The Reptiles—Tuatara creatures, once inhabiting Earth

~*~

**Glossary of Terms found after page 199.**

Chapter One

*Present day Earth, Colorado Springs, Colorado*

Portence Goodeve marched through the underbrush as if leading a military charge. It was hard to believe she was finally going to meet this Lance Lawson guy—her new partner—not that she wanted one, once had been enough. It was the principal of the thing.

She glanced around, her field of vision limited by the thick stand of fir trees through which she navigated. At least meeting Dr. Lawson on the combat practice field beat the heck out of meeting in a stuffy office, or worse yet a hospital—where she'd spent entirely too much time lately.

Cheyenne Mountain would have been her first choice, of course. Touring the facility, a likely Reptile target, topped her current list of things to do—job-wise. Her personal list started and ended with only one name and one mission.

She shoved a branch out of the way and wondered what the good doctor would be like. The perfect combination of military and medicine, or so she'd been told. Gees, another doctor in the mix. It was starting to sound like a Mensa reunion. Okay, so what if her new partner was a geek? Her sister's geek partner, Dr. Nate Calhoun, had turned out to be a great guy—for a human. But see, that was the other thing. Her new partner was not only a brainiac, he was also a human. Probably just as well. She'd sworn off humans, or Humes as the Fae usually referred to the species. No possibility of romantic entanglements, planned or accidental. No possibility for a conflict of interest regarding who she served. She trusted no one who wasn't a full-blooded Fae, especially with her heart.

But screw all this speculating and contemplating. Action is what she wanted and needed. After surviving being poisoned, she'd come back stronger, her endurance greater, her muscles redefined. The new improved model of herself—Portence Rebuilt. And ever since leaving the hospital and getting her mojo back, she'd thought of little else but securing the planet, and tracking down every last one of those scaly *Reptoads*. She gave a little laugh, enjoying her new word for the Reptiles.

Wanting to get the meeting over and done with, she walked a little faster, reminding herself to stay focused, and to just *do the job*. Back in the old days, those three words had gotten her through many an unimaginable situation. It would keep her strong now, too.

Raised voices, drifting on the breeze, grabbed her attention. She clicked on her hypervision, but until she cleared the dense forest, visual confirmation remained impossible. Now the sound of moaning and crying overrode the original voices. She quickened her pace. What the heck was going on? Had there been a Rep attack? When she said she wanted action, she hadn't meant right this fricking minute.

Shedding her heavy jacket, she jogged forward, reconfiguring her silver bracelets into body armor for her hands and forearms. Always best to be prepared.

Particle laser at the ready, she picked up the pace once again, dodging tree trunks and branches. The black long-sleeved top she'd worn beneath her jacket helped to deflect the prickly pine boughs. Nearly there, almost to the edge of the forest. Activating her wingports, she unfurled a set of battle wings, the edges rimmed in metal spikes. They tore through the fabric of her top like it wasn't there. Another piece of her wardrobe ruined.

Battle adrenaline pumped through her veins, and running flat out she grew taller, her ears went pointy, and her muscles grew taut. Clearing the field of trees, she cloaked her image and shot straight into the air to hover and assess. Injured victims were scattered across the practice field. Blue blood stained the bandages and ground—only blue blood, no green for Reptile, or red for human.

Her heart seemed to stop, then trip forward double time. The wounded must be Fae Warriors, but how could that be possible? Were her sisters, Solace and Bliss, among the casualties? Except for the three of them, there were no members of the Fae Warrior Alpha Team assigned to this sector. *It can't be them. It couldn't be them.* The words screamed through her brain as she dipped in for a closer look.

Forcing herself to think logically, she surveyed the surrounding area, searching for the velociraptor-like mercenaries she was itching to take-on. Where were the scaly Fae-eating lunk-heads? Not getting a visual, or detecting the gagging smell of wounded Reptile, she hit the ground running and flash-moved to the center of the action. What was going on? Those rendering aid appeared to be Earth hospital personnel, but something wasn't right. She dropped cover, startling several nearby people. They gained their feet, mouths agape.

"Who's in command here?" she thundered.

Silence fell over the entire group, and they stopped as if frozen in place. All but one person—a large, broad-shouldered, male Hume. Dressed in hospital scrubs, he strode forward, but with his military haircut, steely-eyed glare, and take charge attitude, he seemed more suited for snuffing out a life rather than saving one.

"Sweet Mother of God," he said, coming to stand before her.

"Not sweet and nobody's mother," she shot back, a prick of sadness mingled with her anger.

Standing tall, wings at attention, she challenged his over six-foot-frame, meeting him eye-to-eye. "What the hell's going on here?"

"You're magnificent," he continued, as if not hearing her words. "Just look at her," he murmured to those now gathered near. "This, my weary colleagues, is why you have been training so hard. Why I have pushed you to the limits." He walked around her, checking her out as if she were an animal up for auction. It made her want to gnash her teeth. Instead she flapped her wings, and scoffed when he had to sidestep out of the way.

The *patients* were up and walking around, bandages and IV tubes dangling, medical equipment abandoned and ignored. They weren't Fae, and they weren't injured. A heads-up on what they were doing here today would have been nice, and would have saved her a near heart attack because she thought Solace and Bliss had been injured. As he came back around full-circle, she jabbed a finger into his rock-hard chest, bringing him up short.

"Hold on there, buddy. Who are you?"

"Forgive me. You must be Portence Goodeve. I'm Dr. Lawson, but please call me Lance."

One female *patient*, standing behind him, sighed and glanced adoringly at Lawson.

Port snapped her battle wings shut and eighty-sixed them, sending up a cloud of dust. Well wasn't that just dandy. What was Mother thinking? She'd been partnered up with *McStudly*. While being a patient herself at the clinic, she'd heard about doctors like him. The staff had constantly played the TV in her room, and like it or not, she'd been forced to binge-listen to reruns of a hospital show influenced by some medical book. Using this data as a reference to human behavior, *McStudly* seemed to be the correct nomenclature for this quintessential jock. What an arrogant asswagon.

"Well, *Lance*, I repeat, what the hell is going on?"

As if finally perceiving her anger, he took a step back. "Carry on everyone," he instructed those standing around gawking. "Follow me, Miss Goodeve."

As she did just that, she fought the urge to insist he call her Major Goodeve, her true rank, and a fact unknown to her sisters. They'd never let her live it down. Besides, her rise up the promotional ladder had occurred while doing Special Ops. More secrets to which her sisters were not privy.

He led her to a tent, held the flap aside, and waited for her to enter. Her adrenaline evened out, but the flush of being in combat-mode still warmed her cheeks and blood, making the chilly autumn temperature a welcome relief. A couple of deep breaths helped to calm her thoughts.

She supposed she should be thankful, not so angry. Lately she had one incredibly short fuse, not a good thing for a civilian or a warrior. These Humes were obviously training hard to learn about caring for Fae in emergency situations—she could at least respect the endeavor.

Slouching down onto the camp chair he offered, she returned her new partner's stare as he took the chair across from her. If he was waiting for her to get the ball rolling, they could be here all day.

"I knew you were coming, but you still took me by surprise. You're the first Fae I've met, and in warrior mode to boot. It was just too much."

"You're telling me you have no practical experience healing my kind."

"Well, since we couldn't very well go around doing unnecessary operations just for the fun of it, we've focused on theoretical surgical situations. I know you've been ill, and I'm sorry none of our trauma expertise could be of use. But as we are at war, first-responder techniques and emergency surgery seemed the areas upon which to concentrate."

"Makes sense," she grudgingly agreed. But it also meant they'd be using a Fae for practice if one got injured.

"In addition, the U.S. Army E.T. Squad is taking on more and more human soldiers. They may need a helping hand as well. But never fear, we're expressly here to see to you…your kind…you guys. That sounded rude somehow."

His initial surprise and excitement seemed to have waned, and his previously wide eyes drooped a bit as he considered her. "We've had over half a century to contemplate, investigate, and cogitate what happened in Roswell, and every day seems to bring a new science fiction book or movie, but casually accepting the presence of extraterrestrial beings still comes hard."

"Yeah, I know the feeling. Humans seem pretty alien to us too."

He ran one hand across his face then down his chin as if to wipe away the fatigue evidenced by the slope of his shoulders. He remained silent, and on closer inspection, the buzz-cut he wore failed to hide the gray in his hair, indicating he was quite a bit older than she initially thought.

Grabbing a canteen, he opened it and took a long drink, then offered it to her. Accepting, she downed a healthy swig and handed it back.

"Being a soldier, and a doctor, and a human, I'm the liaison, or hub in this gloriously twisted amalgam of warfare and healthcare. So if you have any questions, I'm your guy. We're pretty well set up now, but the vetting process for personnel took longer than expected."

She didn't doubt it for a minute.

"We're also working on a helicopter landing pad so injured Fae can be shuttled in from outlying areas. God willing, we won't have need of it."

He said all this with great pride, but without conceit or arrogance, and his humble attitude elevated *McStudly's* status to *McMight Have Possibilities* as a partner. For him to be in charge of all this, he had to be at least a lieutenant general.

"Sounds like Mother made a good choice when she picked you for the job," she praised.

He shrugged. "Time will tell."

As the cold set in, an unstoppable shiver cascaded down her spine. Dr. Lawson grabbed a quilted camo jacket and tossed it to her. It fit well, and felt old school and familiar.

"The portable MRI machine arrived yesterday," he extolled. "I've never seen one so small. I'm sure it will prove indispensable working in the field."

He continued expounding on various pieces of medical equipment and procedures, but her mind began to wander. As long as he knew how to use this stuff, she really didn't care. Being a warrior, she had no time for anything else. It's what made her who she was. It's what kept her going, for better or for worse.

*For better or worse.* Which had won out or was she a permutation of both? Had Mother Nature done her a favor or a disservice accepting her application to the SCI? For nearly ten years, Space Counter Intelligence had been her all-consuming life. It had been exhilarating, testing her on every level, physically and mentally. It had also broken her on both. But she had healed completely—almost.

The military had given her life structure, and kept her busy, leaving little time for wallowing in the past, or wasting time dreaming about the future. The trick would be preventing both the past and the future from screwing up the present.

During her current assignment, she'd been shot at, almost blown to smithereens, and poisoned near to death. Of course, considering the mission, these events were not totally unexpected.

But now *he* was somewhere on the planet, which meant her heart and soul were in jeopardy as well. The

Earth might be heading for a Reptile Armageddon, but as far as Portence was concerned, her old partner Malachi was the biggest threat of all.

****

Port headed back to HQ—on the wing. During the day, other than emergencies, unauthorized flying was forbidden, but she felt like breaking some rules. She stayed low, just above tree level, hovering then moving on as she tried to spot her cast-off jacket. The day had turned chilly, and she'd returned the camo gear Dr. Lawson had lent her. Besides, cool-looking pleather bomber jackets were hard to find, and she'd be darned if she'd leave it behind. Once she found the garment, she'd be out of here in a flash and back at the ranch.

Nate, her sister's partner, had arranged for them to stay at his rural property. Strategically located southwest of the Colorado Springs, yet north of Cheyenne Mountain, the arrangement worked out perfectly for Solace, Tanner, Bliss, and herself. Tanner's Army E. T. squad even bivouacked there on occasion. She thought of Dr. Lawson's group. The nearby location tied everything together. Good thing they were close. His group seemed vulnerable out here, with minimal military backup on hand.

Recent aerial recon showed the Reps were scattered about in the forest near the Twin Peaks Dam, which was why the Army couldn't just drop a bomb on the area to end the invasion in this sector. If the dam broke it could kill thousands of Humes.

On the other hand, without containment, the scaly rep-toads were bound to explore—even in this direction. They had adapted well to lying low and living off the land, and Mother warned more were coming.

Once their numbers grew, they would gather together, and the real war would begin. Why else would Malachi be here?

At the mere thought of the sorcerer, the tattoo on her chest, just above her left breast, tingled. Was he thinking of her too? While she lay unconscious in the hospital, Malachi had presumed to mark her with Eolh, the rune sign for protection. Being only half-sorcerer, Malachi had risked much. Not that she cared. He'd also saved her life that night—yet her anger overrode her thankfulness. She hadn't had contact with him since, but she knew he was here.

Pressing the fingertips of one hand to the tattoo, she tried to quiet the irritating reminder of him and what they once shared. It didn't work.

Spying her jacket, she swooped down to ground level, concentrating on dodging branches and tree trunks. Then as she bent to retrieve the garment, a bullet whizzed past where her head had been.

Damn!

Wings dematerialized, she hunkered down, and slipped into the reclaimed outerwear. With her laser pistol in hand, safety off and set to magnum load, she crawled to the right and peeked over a fallen tree to see who was trying to kill her. Dressed in scrubs and holding a Beretta M9, a Hume stood about twenty yards away. She remembered him from the practice field. He'd hung back away from the others. Why would he shoot at her? Could he be a transformed Reptile?

Since the scaly Fae-eaters no longer prowled around the cities, the Reps had given up using the body altering serum. Of course, there had to be a cache of it lying around, so why not occasionally send in one of

10

their kind to do a little spying. But Dr. Lawson said they vetted everybody. Still, it would be easy enough to slip in and nose around for a day or two. She hadn't smelled him coming, so they must still be using the pills to mask their stench. If he was a Rep, he'd stink plenty once she blasted him.

The visual through the branches didn't offer a clean shot, and if he turned out to be a Hume, there'd be hell to pay if she killed him outright. Besides, Hume or Rep, wounding and interrogating him would be the optimal approach. Another bullet smacked into the tree to her left. Then again, accidents happened. Taking aim, she squeezed the trigger.

The blast sheared off a branch and continued onward, hitting her enemy in the left shoulder. He howled in rage, and grabbed at something slung across his back. That something turned out to be an AK 47.

Letting loose with a spate of bullets, he peppered the area around her. Then he dodged sideways through the forest, and glimpses of him between trees and brush became a time-lapse to his metamorphosis. By Jupiter, he was a Rep. As he grew larger, the scrubs he wore burst at the seams and fell away to reveal the real monster hiding beneath the Hume form. She followed his movements, always keeping him in front of her. He halted in a patch of sun. The light glinted off his scaly body, accentuating the ripples of his now muscle-bound form. Why was he just standing there?

About to move in closer, an alarm went off in the back of her mind. This was too easy. She looked over her shoulder just as she heard the rustling of leaves. There were two of them. The one at her back wore camo pants and combat boots, with belts of amo crisscrossed over his expansive scaly chest. He laughed, deep and guttural, and carried the same weaponry as his partner. Bounding forward as if on a suicide mission, he covered the ground quickly, his tooth filled jaws snapping open and closed. She couldn't deploy wings or flash move in the dense trees. Nothing left to do but blast her way out. Good thing she'd recharged her laser last night.

The first shot disabled his rifle. The second tore into his shoulder, creating little effect other than producing a terrible stench as he grabbed his sidearm. The third opened his gut. Green blood splattered the ground and internal organs dangled from the opening. He maintained an upright position for a moment, but the bullets fired from his handgun went wide. Then the weapon dropped from his hand, and his body dropped to the ground.

Holding her breath, she stepped closer and lasered off his head. The Reps could regenerate various pieces of anatomy—arms, legs, tail—but once the mind and body parted company, there was no coming back.

Zigzagging through the trees to a pile of boulders on the edge of the forest, she searched for the first Rep she'd encountered. He was close and heading her way. The bullets he fired zinged off the surrounding stones, creating sparks as they hit metallic particles imbedded in the strata. Not bothering to take cover, as if he too were on a do or die mission, this Rep showed no concern for his own safety. Even for mercenaries it went against the natural instinct for survival. After all, one of them could have kept her pinned down while the other went for reinforcements. In doing so both could have remained alive. It was a poor decision, but it was theirs.

She cloaked her image, stood up, and fired directly into the gaping mouth of the Rep standing barely ten feet away. The back of his scaly finned head blew off, sending green blood and matching brains splattering onto the trees and rock. The rest of his body continued its previous trajectory, and she dove to one side just in time. His lifeless form shook the ground as it hit and tumbled past. His tail, a weapon in itself, flipped wildly through the air grazing her shoulder. The lethal appendage sliced open her jacket and shirt, and she clamped a hand over the burning flesh. As badly as it hurt, she knew she'd been lucky—she could have lost an arm.

Grabbing hold of a boulder, she gained her feet, dropped the cloaking tactic, and trailed after the Rep's body. He rolled to a stop, and that old familiar odor returned ten thousand fold. Although it hardly seemed necessary, she followed procedure and lasered a line across his neck, detaching the mutilated head.

Forcing her pulse and respirations to slow, she stepped away and stood listening—Fae ears erect and on full alert. Had these two been traveling alone? The Rep's gunfire would have been heard for miles. Hypervision on, she scanned the surrounding area. No hot spots.

The forest remained silent. She clicked off the visual enhancement, and retrieved her hand held. She should update Tanner on the situation. Solace's partner, Captain Tanner Jackson was ex-Army Ranger, and his select group of Humes were privy to the fact aliens were on the planet—information shared by only a few. He should run a recon patrol through here, and maybe leave some of his men with Dr. Lawson's group.

As she waited for Captain Jackson to pick up, she backtracked over to the first kill, squatted down, and rifled through the pockets of his camo cargo pants.

Well…this is interesting.

Chapter Two

On the way back to headquarters, Port contacted her sisters. Better to fill them in before Tanner could. This way she could play down the danger. After she had nearly died from the bio-agent poisoning, things between the three sisters had changed.

Of the triplets, the role of big sister had always been hers. Although only by a matter of minutes, she was the first born, so it only seemed fitting. She also refereed the infighting, and they always deferred to her in a tie situation. Now Solace and Bliss worried about her—actually worried—as if she needed protecting. It was ludicrous and annoying. She outranked them, had been in SCI, and she didn't like answering to anyone.

As she entered the woodsy cabin serving as their office, she tried to look nonchalant. Bliss remained seated, but set aside the arrow she fletched. Not meaning to, Port winced as she hung up her jacket.

"You're hurt worse than you said," Solace accused, gaining her feet.

"Relax," she reassured her, flicking pine needles from the jacket which had saved her from worse injury. "It's nothing major." Then trying not to grimace and limp in response to her aching muscles, she went to the mini-fridge, grabbed a banana Popsicle, and eased down onto a chair by the table.

For their own safety, her sisters deserved to hear

more about the encounter, so before they could badger her into a full-blown recital, she motioned for Solace to sit down. Then she offered up her modified version

"And," she said in conclusion, "this is what one of them was carrying."

Retrieving the items from her pockets, Port tossed them on the table.

Solace poked at the pile. "Hume money—quite a bit. Car keys and a burner cell phone. Sounds like these guys were on a road trip."

"I think they were AWOL. One of them had whip marks on his scaly green back. Maybe things at the enemy camp aren't all fun and games. The Reps are no longer free agents running amuck and doing as they please. They're more organized, and that means someone is keeping them under control, someone even meaner and scarier than they are."

As she shifted in her chair, pain shot through her body, ending with a throbbing ball of fire in her injured shoulder.

"What a dreadful thought," Bliss said, as she rummaged around in one of her famous totes. "Here sis, you may want this later." She set a tube of Saturnalia cream on the table, no nagging or making a big deal out of it, just Bliss being kind, and knowing by her empath skills Port was hurting big time.

"Does Tanner know you found this stuff?" Solace asked.

"Yes. I phoned him from the scene, but he ordered me not to wait, and I didn't want to risk this evidence disappearing. I told him about the car keys, and he's hoping to find the vehicle they were supposedly going to use."

"This is the strangest war I've ever been in," Solace mused. "First, the enemy is running around disguised as the good guys, and now when we have a basic idea where they are, we aren't allowed to ferret them out for fear of injuring Humes or blowing up the damn dam."

"I don't like waiting either," Port agreed. "But I've a feeling something's going to give and soon."

"So how'd your first meeting with *the* Dr. Lawson go?" Bliss asked, getting around to the more mundane.

"I didn't hate him."

Solace burst out laughing, slapping her open palm on the table. Bliss groaned, pretending to be upset.

"I told you she'd say that," Solace hooted. "Pay up Bliss, you owe me five thousand Earth dollars."

"Okay, okay. Here you go."

It was Port's turn to be concerned. She glanced from one to the other then grinned as her redheaded sister counted out rainbow colored Monopoly money. They'd found the game on a shelf in the cabin, and had been using the contents to play Hands Down, a game similar to the Earth game Craps—which made her think of the crap-eating Megaderms—which reminded her of being left on the trash planet by Malachi.

Her smile faded. No matter what barriers she thought she had in place, Malachi invaded her thoughts. Was he doing it by magic, or was she betraying herself?

"So what's Nate up to today?" she asked, focusing on something else—anything else.

Bliss' partner, Nathaniel Calhoun, was a brainiac/cowboy. And besides owning the land upon which they *bivouacked* and called their headquarters, he liked tinkering with and inventing weaponry and other curious gadgets.

An eclectic group, they worked well together. The proof being they'd thwarted a NOAA takeover scheme, eliminated three high-level Reptile operatives, and seized a big old batch of bio-agent toxin which Mother had since destroyed. Not to mention eliminating a money laundering operation and a drug/sex trafficking ring. Sadly, they hadn't been able to save all the young women preyed upon. At least Mother had made sure little Troika's remains were returned to her family and her homeland. Family was important.

A shudder twisted through her at the thought of the poison. She'd nearly died from it, and had crossed paths with *him* because of it. There she went again. All roads did not lead to Rome, they led to Malachi. Finished with her Popsicle, she flung the stick at the recycle bin.

"Nate's working on yet another experiment," Bliss said. "Now tell us more about Dr. Lawson. You didn't hate him and…?"

Solace stared at her too, with great expectation, waiting for her to say more. She owed them big time for taking such good care of her when she was down. Yet anxiety dogged her steps, night and day, and she felt restless for no good reason, making her gritchy to live with. But her sisters meant the world to her, and she never wanted to hurt them. Better get with the program.

"The meeting went fine. Really. And we're going to tour the frickin' mountain tomorrow."

Afraid if she sat still too long she'd stiffen up, Port gained her feet and paced about in front of the Army tactical board. The Fae Warriors Mother board stood beside it. Created ethereally by Mother Nature their board hovered about five feet off the ground, and although devoid of wires, transmitters, or a power source of any kind, it connected to all the other high-tech equipment. The sisters could update it from here, and Mother could update it from wherever she happened to be. Right now the board stood empty.

"What's on our docket for the rest of today?" she asked.

"We trained until we dropped this morning," Solace said, her long black hair still twisted into a knot on top of her head.

"Other than that, it's been suspiciously quiet," Bliss added. "We're sitting tight and waiting for orders." A sheaf of her long red hair spilled forward as she reached down to scratch the neck of the huge shaggy beast asleep and snoring at her feet. "Even Noodge has been lackadaisical this afternoon."

Noodge was a Rapran, short for Rapacious Ranivorous, a reptile eating alien creature. Mother had given him to the sisters to aid their military efforts, but he had soon become an endearing pet as well as a lethal weapon. Larger than a tiger, faithful as a Tibetan mastiff, and rambunctious as a black tailed wallaby he earned his keep tracking and destroying Reptile enemies. Bliss, with her empath skills, had the most control over him, but he'd found a place in all their hearts.

Port sighed and kept pacing, and coming around full circle once more, she toyed with her braid, checking the tip for split ends. Following her near death experience with the bio-agent, her once pure white hair now sported streaks of light blue—unexpected and unique, and so far permanent.

The three sisters were identical accept for the color

of their hair, their philosophies of life, and what turned them on regarding the male species. Bliss and Solace had found Humes to share their hearts and their beds, but Portence remained determined to go it alone. She really had no choice. Although she wanted nothing more to do with Malachi, after what she had once known with him, all other liaisons fell sadly short. If she couldn't find that kind of love again, she'd go without.

Halting, Port stared out the window. Bliss' idea of sitting tight sounded like torture. Maybe she should take a ride on her assigned horse, Mouse. The Fae loved riding like the wind, and thanks to Nate, there were equine available for leisure, or for transportation while scouting the surrounding rough terrain.

"You okay, Port?" Solace asked.

Turning, she smiled and studied her sisters, overwhelmed by the love she felt for them. Although their connection wavered on occasion, right now, it was as strong as it had been when they were together as children—before being separated. Since then, they had all seen plenty of action, and they all knew what was coming. But now they worried not only about themselves, but also about each other.

"I'm good. I'm going to hit the showers." In retrospect, soothing hot water sounded like a better idea than jostling along on a horse. "I'll catch up with you guys at supper."

They seemed disappointed in her not hanging out and talking with them, but sometimes chitchat got on her nerves, and the need for space and solitude kept nagging at her.

Crossing the yard, she headed for the ranch house

and her room. When she glanced at the nearby pond, a flashback from her stint in the hospital hit Port with a jolt. Although she was unconscious and couldn't respond, every evening when her little British night nurse tucked her in, she promised Port would soon be playing ducks and drakes, meaning she'd be well and happy and skipping stones across the water. The image had been so endearing it had actually comforted her. She'd heard those words night after night, had clung to them, had believed in them. But now, she didn't think it would apply to her anytime soon.

## Chapter Three

The new day dawned cold, but Malachi's blood ran hot.

Restraining the words of rebellion screaming across his mind, he gave free rein to the fury he knew blazed in his eyes. Mother Nature's reaction was a raised brow of amusement, as if she dared him to challenge her orders. He'd been called dangerous, even foolhardy, and although royally pissed, he was not stupid. Turning his back, he fought down the resentment and frustration.

"You knew what you were getting into when you signed up with SCI," she reminded him.

"Have you no pity in your heart?" He spun around, his gaze searching her face. "I've done everything you've asked."

"It's your last assignment. Then you're free to do as you please. You know she needed the time, and wouldn't have listened to you before now."

Perhaps. Or had Mother kept him from Portence longer than necessary in order to serve her own purposes? Always a possibly. Still her words had the ring of truth to them, but it only amped up the pain in his soul. To know Portence was near, and to be ordered to leave her alone, seemed a torture beyond any he'd previously endured. This might be one command he would have to disobey.

Trying to override the words he longed to say, he rolled his shoulders, stretching the tight muscles of his back and neck. He felt like a caged tiger, ready to spring, ready to fight whoever or whatever got in his way—again—except for Mother.

"You're my eyes and ears, Malachi, on what may be one of the most important missions of your life. An entire planet is at stake. I realize you don't give a tinker's damn about these humans, but I do. They can be selfish and shortsighted, and don't realize what a gift they've been given to live on Earth, but they can also be humorous and compassionate and even noble on occasion."

"If you say so." As of yet, he hadn't crossed paths with any of the humans on this distant planet, far from his home.

"You're one of my best. I know you won't fail me."

He gave a snort of sarcasm at her attempt at flattery, but in the end knew he would bow to her will—bow to honor, and keep the oath he'd taken. A sorcerer's word was a sacrosanct bond. Besides, who was he to judge Mother Nature, the ruler of the Multiverse? A position which no doubt came with an inconceivable set of problems, forcing hard decisions and leaving little room for sentiment.

In all fairness, Mother had treated him well. She'd seen to his being sanctioned to study his craft with the most famous mystics and wizards available. He was near to achieving level ten, a privilege never before granted to anyone other than a purebred sorcerer. She'd also fed his desire for adventure with assignments crisscrossing the galaxies where he'd been allowed to practice and wield his powers—for the good.

*Only his mission with Portence had been a disaster.*

He supposed that wasn't Mother's fault either. Malachi guessed he wanted to find someone to blame other than himself for how things had turned out. Although to be honest, after reliving the nightmare in his mind countless times, he still didn't know what he would have done differently.

"Just so you are aware"—he pointed out—"the situation here has become vexing to the point of being nearly unbearable."

Mother had assigned him to play nursemaid and psychoanalyst to Xandora, and he'd followed the irrational female across the galaxy, reporting back to Mother as requested. But now, regardless of what he'd originally promised the Goddess and Multiverse, the chance of making amends with Portence changed everything—no matter how remote the likelihood. In the future there would be no satisfying Xandora in any intimate capacity.

The act had been selfish and demanding on Xandora's part, and perfunctory on his, like eating or drinking. There had certainly been no affection involved in carrying out the chore, and from this point forward, it would not be repeated. He'd gone three long years without Portence, and without hope of ever seeing her again. These new circumstances changed everything. Now, he needed all this to be over so he could go on with his life, or more accurately, so it could truly begin again—with the only female he'd ever loved.

"I realize Xandora's special to you," he said, taking

another tact, "but I can't be responsible for the silly twit much longer. She's coming off the rails one wheel at a time, yet remaining cognizant enough to realize her world takeover plan begins and ends with this North American country.

"Her Reptile drill sergeant, as well as Thurax, the demon she's put in charge of the overall operation, have arrived. She'll soon be mustering her forces. Yesterday, she had me use my skills to shuttle her highness to several strategic points around the globe. I wasn't privy to what she discussed with her various Rep leaders, but once she gives the signal, the fact reptiles have invaded the Earth will no longer be a secret, and pandemonium will no doubt ensue."

"So noted. But I need the intel to which you *do* have access, and I need you to protect Xandora—from herself if necessary. I shut down the portal she hijacked to the outer realms. Now only a god could break through the security around it. I'm sorry your nemesis got through before I realized what she'd done."

"It doesn't matter. Thurax and I have a date with destiny, it might as well be here. So far we've kept our distance from one another, relying on sneering and trash talk. But one of us won't leave Earth alive."

"Again, when you're a free agent, you may do as you please. I won't interfere. Just remember, you're special to me, Malachi."

His gaze met hers, and he believed she meant what she said. But when necessary, Mother would always put the good of the Multiverse ahead of everything else.

"And Portence is special to *me*," he reaffirmed. "From now on, she comes first. Don't ever doubt that."

\*\*\*\*

Xandora couldn't decide whom she hated more, her sister Pandora or Mother Nature.

At the moment, she supposed Mother Nature topped the list. Of the two, MoNat was the most dangerous. But she'd outwitted her supreme bitchiness so far, and she intended to keep it that way.

She needed a planet, and she wanted Earth. Such a pretty little twirling orb, Mother's favorite, another reason to have it—or destroy it. The humans, so driven by greed and misplaced religious fervor, would make excellent chattel. After all, what good did it do to rule a planet or acquire power and wealth if you didn't have slaves to worship you like a rock star?

Thanks to the portal she'd temporarily commandeered, her legions had grown considerably. Now they constituted a force not to be ignored, and with the help of her mystic warrior, victory would surely be hers. She would be a true goddess, adored and revered—or she would become Earth's personal demon, unforgiving and feared.

****

Port swallowed hard to stave off another round of panic as she and Dr. Lawson sped along the winding two lane road leading to Cheyenne Mountain. Glad now she'd agreed to let him drive, she needed all her concentration just to keep it together. Soon she'd be buried beneath tons of granite—*not buried, just inside*. That sounded good on paper, but it would feel like being buried.

Her fascination of seeing the military wonder had blocked her inbred Fae horror of being underground. The excitement of the subterranean tour had seduced her into thinking the fear could be conquered. But the sneaky phobia had been patiently waiting, and now it showed its fangs.

What was she thinking? This time tested terror went back eons to when Man defeated the wee-folk, sentencing them to live in the nether-world of mounds and burrows. Magic died that day too. Thankfully Mother Nature saved Port's people from the darkness, and now they lived and thrived on Kepler 186f. They owed Mother much, and Port would never forget it—but Mother owed her too. For the first time in her long life, she was rather PO'd with Mother. Why had she brought Malachi here?

"You okay?" Lance asked, with a sideways glance.

At the sound of his voice she gave an involuntary jerk.

"Sorry," he said, "didn't mean to make you jump out of your skin."

"Cripes, I hate that expression."

He gave her a curious look.

"Yes, I've actually seen it happen. It's the only way the inhabitants of Dermis III can sustain life on their disease ridden planet. In one fluid movement, they leap naked in the air, shedding their skin in one complete piece. The process leaves them cleansed of all superficial bugs and viruses they may have come into contact with during the day."

"As a physician I find that fascinating. As a little boy, housed in a grown man's body, I find that friggin' awesome and a bit horrifying."

"It's not that big of a deal. They can only do it once every twenty-four hours."

They rolled to a stop at the armed checkpoint, and got out as instructed. She stared up at the looming gray

Gini Rifkin

wall of rock. All nine thousand feet of it. She could swear it studied her as well. Not maliciously and not friendly but with indifference. The mountain had been there a long time. It was due her respect, as well as her fear.

The guard personally parked their truck then escorted them to a military vehicle which he drove the mile and half to the entrance of the tunnel. The impending opening reminded her of the Zarminian Caves of No Return, or the gaping maw of a sea creature, for surely they headed for the belly of the beast. Stealing her nerves, she stepped from bright Colorado sunshine into the dark roughhewn gullet.

*Focus on the details, don't think about where you are.*

Reminding herself she was a warrior, she noted how the main tunnel split off to the right, bringing them to the first set of blast doors. Instructed to wait, she fidgeted and glanced around. Artificial light bounced off rock and steel creating a deceptively warm glow. If the power went out, there wouldn't be any glow, fake or otherwise.

A middle-aged man, wearing fatigues and an air of authority, strode forward.

"I'm Colonel Stewart, commander of the 721st Mission Support Group," he announced. "We run Cheyenne Mountain, and with the help of the folks at NORAD we keep the airspace over North America safe. I take it you're Lawson and Goodeve?" he asked, giving them the once-over.

"Affirmative," Lance said, taking the lead. He'd also worn Army gear today, making a good showing of his own. She couldn't wish for a better Hume partner.

He had lots of old school smarts, and so far he seemed easy to get along with. And it didn't hurt he seemed intrigued by everything Fae.

Although of equal rank, the two men respectfully saluted one another before shaking hands. When the Colonel reached for hers, he held rather than shook it as his piercing analytical gaze bore into hers.

She'd heard several urban legends about alien creatures, alive and dead, being housed in this mountain—not quite an Area 51, but close. The scenarios ran the gambit, questioning whether the aliens were here to help, here to cause chaos, or if they were being held against their will. Maybe the commander didn't find it so hard to comprehend she was an alien as well. But it would be good to know exactly where he stood on the subject.

"Thank you for personally showing us around today," she said, reclaiming her hand. "I believe you've been informed regarding my status and what we're up against. Any questions or problems with any of this?" she challenged. Hey, she belonged to Mother Nature's Fae Warrior Alpha Team, not the US Military complex. She intended to present a strong front of her own, getting the message out—*nobody messed with or told the Fae what to do*.

He gave a little smile and relaxed his stance. "Our operations have been bi-national for years. Americans and Canadians," he explained. "And we've an eye turned globally as well. I don't see why we can't be bi-planet or bi-species or whatever this is being labeled. Seems it was bound to happen eventually, I welcome it. But I would prefer to keep personnel here on a need to know basis."

"A good idea," she agreed. "In fact we would insist upon it."

She didn't, however, agree with his cavalier attitude regarding worlds colliding. There were places, things, and entities out there of which no human dreamed of in his worst nightmare. Colliding with them was not recommended.

The Colonel motioned them down the tunnel then followed after, halting when they reached the open area between the two sets of blast doors. It reminded her of an airlock on a space vehicle. Then the door at her back began to swing shut.

She stiffened and spun around. "What's happening, why is that door closing?"

An alarm sounded as the panel sealed off one entrance to the room, and a series of giant pistons slid forward into large corresponding slots.

"Just routine. We do this once a day. It won't take long. Although each door weighs twenty-five tons, we can open or close them in approximately thirty seconds."

The door at the other end began to close as well. Thirty seconds, she could do this. Yet, leaning toward the still open portal, it took all she had to convince herself to keep her feet firmly planted on the ground.

"There are five lakes inside the mountain..." the Colonel droned on, conversationally.

Hands curled into fists, she didn't care about the availability of water. Right now, the amount of air in this particular room seemed way more important. Trying to maintain a normal expression, she focused on sifting through the information she'd learned about Cheyenne Mountain, other than the fact she was entombed inside. A trap door to the outside world existed in one of the tunnels, which tunnel hadn't been indicated, and she doubted the location would be anywhere near her current position.

"We're totally self-sufficient," he lectured, "a small city really, with a clinic, gymnasium, food prep facility, and the ability to generate our own utilities for up to forty-five days."

So they had plenty of food—that sounded hopeful, but not if she couldn't breathe.

"Are you able to shield the interior against an electromagnetic pulse attack?"

The second door swung shut with a doomsday thud.

*Good question Lance.* Her mind had gone numb, she couldn't ask one if she tried. She could only hope to assimilate the Colonel's answer.

"We're the only DOD high-altitude Electromagnetic Pulse certified underground facility. We use wall-mounted EMP filters called metallic-oxide varistors which dampen the pulse. The system also allows personnel inside to break away interior electronics from the external commercial power grid.

"The Mission Support Group is pretty much ready for anything, including medical emergencies, natural disasters, civil disorder, or a cyber information attack."

"How about chemical and biological?"

*Another good question, Lance.* Especially considering the recent poison attack they'd dealt with.

"Of course. We're ready for all such emergencies," the Colonel reassured. "Chemical, radiological, improvised, or a general nuclear attack. The security here is level one, more secure than the Pentagon.

"What was that?" She glanced around, and swore the building moved.

"Not to worry." The Colonel's face took on the expression of a proud parent. "Nothing can touch us down here. The interior buildings are free standing, sitting on over one thousand giant springs, absorbent enough to handle an explosion or earthquake."

She admired his confidence, but didn't share it. "Mountains are alive. If you don't respect them, they will make you do so."

Ancient tales of the dark times wrapped around her. She recalled childhood stories about her ancestors dying and pleading their case in the hall of the Crimson King. Permission to leave had been cruelly denied, and her people were forced to remain within the underground realm. Without sunlight they began to waste away.

Eventually, rather than hate the mountain, her tribe had decided to honor the place that would become their tomb. The mountain heard their prayers. A large slab of rock broke loose, right over the king's thrown, crushing him and starting a civil war. Just as her clan fled for their lives, Mother stepped in, saving her people by taking them to another planet. Port wished Mother would pluck her from this underground death trap.

Lance ambled to her side. "Deep breath and hold onto a button," he whispered out of the side of his mouth. "You know, like when a hearse goes by."

A hearse? This advice hardly eased her fears. Yet, the way he said it with such assurance and concern had her sucking in a big breath and letting it out slowly as she reached for and squeezed the button on her pleather jacket. Trying to figure out what Lance had meant actually helped ratchet down her dread.

After what appeared to be a routine security check, the doors opened in sync, and polite or not, she was the first one out. The Colonel caught up with her and led the way to the inner command center. Although day to day procedures were run over at Peterson Air Force Base, the room made an impression—crowded with computers, two seven foot vid screens, and several smaller monitors.

The rest of the tour, thankfully short, reassured them an assault to overthrow and take the mountain by a frontal attack would be futile. If time allowed, a good old fashion siege might work, but it would take months. There was no way the Reptiles were going to make this their global headquarters any time soon.

\*\*\*\*

As they drove back to Nate's property, Port lowered her window on the passenger side of Lance's 4x4 truck, and gulped in fresh cool air. "How did you know I have underground claustrophobia?"

"You remind me of my daughter. She's about your age."

"Oh really. She's over two hundred years old?"

"Okay, let me rephrase that. She's about the age you appear to be. Anyway, when she was eleven years old, we toured a cave, like Cave of the Winds right here in Colorado Springs. It's magnificent by the way, filled with stalactites and stalagmites. In fact, it looks like it was made by faeries." He smiled, but right now she didn't appreciate his humor.

"Anyway," he continued, "she begged me to take her, and even though I knew closed-in spaces were not her thing, I relented and we went. About half way through, she had the exact expression on her face you were sporting. I told her the same thing, and it seemed to help her relax and make it through the cave."

"Well, thank you"

"Well, you're welcome. It's what partners do."

"I get the deep breathing bit, but what's with the hold a button like when a hearse goes by?"

He gave a hardy laugh. "Sorry, I guess the superstition from my Midwestern upbringing isn't as well-known as I thought. Back in my day, if you saw a hearse go by, you grabbed a button to make sure you weren't the next to die. Recalling the old belief made my daughter laugh, and took her mind off the walls closing in."

"Where is she now?"

"She's a marine biologist. Out on assignment near the Sulu Archipelago islands. Every time I say Sulu, it makes me think of Star Trek."

"I remember reading about that Earth TV show. Beam me up Scotsman."

"Scotty."

"What?"

"Never mind. I worry about her being out to sea."

"The way things are going on dry land, she may be in the safest place on Earth."

****

The Sisters of Anu, plus Tanner, Nate, and Lance crowded around the war table in the cabin, each grasping a mug of either coffee or tea. Noodge chewed contentedly on his motor cycle tire. Owing to the fact it was just after midnight, they were each a little bleary-eyed, but they'd managed to devour the mega-snacks Alfonso whipped up on the spur of the moment. Nate's compadre and houseman, kept them fueled on delicious meals, making them wish never to see another MRE.

When the Mother board came alive with a crackle and snap, Port jumped along with everyone else. Then a live picture of a constellation she couldn't place filled the screen. Mother usually phoned in her battle plans and instructions. This time was different.

"Greetings, children." Mother's voice, so loud and clear, seemed to come from every corner of the room. Noodge glanced up and cocked his head to one side. "Sorry to roust you out of bed, but I'll be busy elsewhere shortly and need to bring you up to speed as to who is in charge of the Reptiles, and this invasion. Her name is Xandora, and I'm not pleased." At the heated tone in her voice, everyone seemed to shrink down in their chairs.

"Recently, she managed to open a restricted portal which allowed more Reptiles to come through at a faster rate and therefore in greater numbers. Scuttlebutt from home also indicates she's propositioned a few deities to back her project, and then there's magic to be considered."

Magic—did she mean Malachi? Portence felt as if she'd taken an arrow to the heart, and her tattoo prickled adding annoyance to her pain.

Glancing around the room, she noticed Tanner, Nate, and Lance, appeared confused and completely out of their element. "Xandora is Pandora's sister," Solace tried to explain, although this didn't appear to clear up anything for the three men.

"For the safety of civilian life, it's time we considered evacuating Colorado Springs and the surrounding area," Mother continued. "I'll leave the details up to you as to how this is accomplished. We know this sector is a main target, and collateral damage will be high if we aren't prepared. I'll give you every assist possible. Unfortunately, there's a difference between my assuring the field of battle being fair, and my taking sides. I have petitioned the Council, but have not been granted authority to personally participate in combat. Gaia, Mother Earth, will of course do what she can.

"Any ETA on when the real battle will begin?" Tanner asked.

"We should have a few days, a week at most. From both perspectives it's a massive undertaking. I'll do my best to keep you updated. They're now gathering in a canyon at the foot of Twin Peaks dam."

"I thought Xandora was in prison some place," Solace said.

"She was. Operative word *was*. After Pandora remanded herself to a cloister to atone for opening the jar—as if it was her fault—Xandora hooked up with Pandora's philandering husband, Epimetheus. The silly Titan encouraged Xandora's wild ways, and in a fit of rage and desire for unresolved retribution, she stormed Olympus in an attempt to take Zeus hostage. The plan failed, of course, and Xandora was captured and sentenced to a rehabilitation planet. She soon escaped, again with the help of Epimetheus. Since then she's been busy, and she's as uncontrollable as she is untiring. I rue the day…" Mother's angry tone trailed off into a rumble of thunder.

All Fae children knew about Xandy and Pandy. There was even a fictional book about their notorious adventures and hijinks. Port had seen paintings of the two sisters—Pandora was stunning, Xandora was less attractive but not without charm. Was Malachi working with this treacherous sub-goddess—and was he playing with her too?

"Anybody else we should know about?" Bliss asked, breaking the palpable silence.

"Yes. Hephaestus, having created Pandora, never lost contact with her, and by association he's connected to Xandora. With his yen for weaponry, we believe she may ask him to supply arms for her cause. And while the Reptiles constitute her main strength, she's recruited a few mercenary creatures from across the Multiverse. She wasn't idle while in captivity, and now having gained her freedom, anything is possible."

Port wondered if everyone else's pulse rate just quickened. The scenario sounded pretty grim, but they'd all been through worse. To be honest, her biggest concern was adjusting to working with the military Humes. They should have done more cross-species team combat training.

"How did this little hellcat manage to hijack a restricted portal, ma'am" Nate asked, with his cowboy drawl.

"Just like the poison previously obtained via Spacebook, with enough money, you can buy almost anything, including the assistance of nefarious galactic entities. Regardless, the portal has now been closed. Stay ready and stay alert. Mother, out."

The screen went blank, and the atmosphere in the room and everyone in it seemed to relax as if a spell had been broken.

"I don't know about Nate and Tanner," Lance put in, "but the addition of myth and magic has me concerned. It wasn't in our game plan when exploring medical and surgical contingencies."

"After Raprans, Reptiles, and Fae Warriors, I suppose we shouldn't be so surprised," Nate said with a grin.

"At least we know in advance," Tanner reassured. "We can deal with it." His words held more bravado than his expression. "If we need backup, as a last resort, we can involve the regular Army," he added, "at least for rearguard support. Hopefully any new troops would be far enough away from the action so as not to have direct contact with the enemy."

"That might work." Solace smiled at her Hume partner. "Although the Reps are taller than humans, in battle gear, they won't look too alien from a distance. And we need to meet them out in the open," she added, stifling a yawn. "Draw them away from the protection of the canyon they're in, and away from the dam. But we should also stock pile for defensive action."

"Agreed." Tanner nodded.

Nate gained his feet and stepped to the map tacked to the wall. "In case we get cut off from the ranch house, I've developed a couple of solar powered rechargers for use with the particle laser pistols and shotguns." He pointed to the blue X marks, one by the barn the other by the entrance to the property. "I'm still working on a more portable one for use in the field."

"Fantastic," Bliss praised.

"Don't forget," Lance reminded, "we must keep our forces between the field hospital and the enemy at all times. If the Reps take over the hospital, there won't be any nearby facility set up for Fae or human emergencies."

Unlike a regular battle, which encouraged guts, glory, and anything goes, taking down the Reps had to be handled more delicately, with concern for the general populace. But this type of warfare put the enemy in charge, which didn't set well with any of them. Port remembered how tricky subversive warfare could be.

Was Malachi making war plans too? Was he thinking of her? She'd found a feather from a red-tail hawk on her windowsill this morning. The bird, his frequent companion, often did his bidding.

\*\*\*\*

With a crystal goblet of ambrosia in one hand, and a platter of elven cookies in the other, Mother Nature eased down onto her velvet fainting couch.

She had existed since the beginning of time—since before the Titans had fought the gods of old and lost. Yet, she hadn't seen this coming. It certainly proved out the theory—no good deed went unpunished.

Looking back, she hadn't seen the harm in Zeus ordering Hephaestus to create Pandora, the first woman. But Zeus had played them false, and rather than an act of kindness, his twisted plan of vengeance was meant to punish Prometheus for stealing fire from Heaven and giving it to Man.

Fashioned from water and clay, Pandora had possessed many gifts. Athena taught her the crafts, Aphrodite gave her beauty, Apollo music, and Hermes persuasion. She was perfect, she was irresistible, but she harbored too darn much curiosity.

Mother took a sip of nectar, and nibbled at the dainty delights. The memory of long ago remained bright in her mind as if it had all played out yesterday.

During the irreverent making of Pandora, discarded bits of matter required to fashion woman numero uno, lay writhing on the ground. They struggled desperately to survive, almost demanding to take on a life of their own. That's when she had allowed pity and compassion to overrule good sense and good judgement.

She'd saved the cast off energy, becoming the biggest unwitting accomplice of them all, and thus Xandora had been born—but not as perfectly as Pandora. Her hair was dark, rather than a lustrous yellow, her eyes a dull brown not China blue. But those eyes could burn bright with the unquenchable desire for glory, and they reflected no conscience.

Physically, Pandora could dance and leap about like a deer in springtime. Xandora limped slightly, especially when she was tired, or when she was angry, which seemed much of the time.

Being lenient with Xandora hadn't helped, and neither had tough love. She seemed destined for destruction, especially her own. And while the two sisters were as different as cold dark matter and hot quasar light, they seemed equally cursed.

The day Pandora opened the jar, the rivalry between the two sisters had begun. Pandora's first act of rebellion had caused all the ills in the world. Xandora's last act may be to use those ills to command the planet or destroy it. Of course Hope remained, cowering in the jar. Although never given the credit, another sticking point, Xandora had slammed the lid shut not Pandora. Now, if Xandora wasn't stopped, she would take over the Earth. Ironically she was cruel enough to rule without allowing the humans the comfort of Hope which she had once saved.

Chapter Four

Port reached for another banana Popsicle, then noticed she hadn't finished the one in her other hand. Slamming the freezer shut, she annihilated the original, and flung the stick at the trash can as if both had personally insulted her.

Today, they'd checked and repaired equipment and practiced their combat skills. Nothing seemed to have changed as far as their enemy. Right now, still in a state of mental turmoil, she remained in the hideaway she'd discovered and went back to pondering.

The spacious pantry, off the kitchen of the main log house, fit her mood—dark and cold, or more precisely, coldhearted. It's what she would have to be to get through this.

Maybe she could call Mother. She'd know where he was. Oh what difference did it make where he was? Malachi wasn't with *her*, what else counted? But the memories wouldn't stop.

She kept reliving what life had been like when they were together. Slapping her hand on her chest, she pressed against the tattoo, but the unwanted ink teased her senses just like he used to tease and enliven other parts of her body. Had he employed magic from the get-go? Maybe she never loved him at all. Maybe a spell had held her entranced, and an incantation created the obsession. All the more reason she should track him down and have it out with him.

Reason—or excuse?

The partially open door to the big pantry swung wide—spilling light into the room. She tensed and squinted at Alfonso, wishing she'd had time to cloak her presence. The phenomenon couldn't be called invisibility, it simply rendered her unseen. There was a difference, but moot at this point.

"Señorita," he began. "If you are hungry I will gladly make you a snack."

Unable to come up with a logical reason for being caught skulking about in the pantry, she remained silent.

"Or perhaps," he said, with a little smile, "you sought the coolness. It is quite warm for this time of year. The welcome relief is hard to resist." Being a true gentleman, he gave her a way out for being found in such an unorthodox place.

"You caught me," she said. "I just finished brushing Mouse and mucking out his stall, and I felt overwhelmed." What a big fat lie. True, she had done those chores, but such light exercise would never tire her, let alone be overwhelming.

"If you are thirsty, there is ice tea and cold lemonade on the front porch. The others are gathered there talking." He strolled about the room selecting items from shelves and containers, putting them into the large basket she just realized he carried. Probably ingredients for tonight's meal.

"Sounds great. Thank you, Alfonso—for everything." Nice of him to let her know where everybody was.

Slipping out the door, she bee-lined it to the empty,

and blessedly silent, back porch.

Evening had arrived since she'd been cooling her heels in the pantry. She glanced at the fading silhouette of the barn. She could hang out with Mouse, or saddle him up. She loved that big dappled gray gelding. But being restricted to the immediate area took the joy out of riding. Mouse needed to run like the wind, not prance around a paddock. He had heart, and seemed all muscle and power—held in check by sculpted beauty. A noble and faithful creature, unlike some sorcerer she knew.

Stepping down from the porch, she stood in the middle of an open patch and stared up at the sky and a trillion/billion stars. A meteorite left a fiery trail across the sky. She started to make a wish then changed her mind. Wishes were for children. Besides, other than wishing for a quick ending to the war they faced, she didn't need anything or anyone.

Deciding to head back to the ranch house, she turned around and ran smack into *him*. Even with Fae ears she hadn't heard his approach. He reached out, gripping her upper arms, steadying her. Wrenching free, she took two steps back.

"What in supersymmetry are you doing here?"

"I came to warn you."

"About what? I don't need your help."

"You needed my help back then, Portence, and you need it now. Why must you always be so stubborn?

"It's poor strategy to bring up what you did to me in the past," she snapped, ignoring his question.

Mouth pressed into a grimace, she stood her ground, fighting to remain calm. Fighting not to slap his face and then fling herself into his arms. They stood in the moonlight staring at one another, he with those golden eyes, clear and penetrating. His expression hot as molten amber.

His five o'clock shadow had slid closer to eight o'clock, deepening the angles of his beautiful face, adding darkness and danger to the sculpted features so angelic when he so chose. His lustrous black hair, grown longer, had been tamed into multiple braids intertwined with feathers and beads, all of it hanging down his back over the hood of the caftan he wore. The long flowing fabric, black as his hair, twinkled with Celtic symbols embroidered in silver thread.

The garb obscured his form except where it stretched tight to accommodate his broad shoulders and chest, but she remembered every dip and hollow of his well-muscled body. She'd touched and tasted of it fully, repeatedly.

"Thurax is here."

His statement hit her like a blunt instrument, bringing her up short, stopping her from telling him to go jump in a fire-lake. Then, for a moment, her mind went blank at the horror inspired by his information.

With a shiver, she glanced around. Why would their old archrival be here? He was the reason she and Malachi had ended up in deep space, fighting for their lives in a broken down clunker of a light-year shuttle. Or was he lying? Squaring her shoulders and shaking off the fear, she stared him down. "Thurax is dead."

"Afraid not. He's a little worse for wear, I'll grant you, but definitely not dead. He's working freelance now."

By Mithras, that ratcheted up the odds in favor of the enemy. Fighting Reptiles hadn't worried her beyond the usual concerns of combat, not that they weren't tough and deadly. But throw in an alien bred for warfare, one who lived and breathed for conquest, this upped the ante. Guess they should be glad he came solo.

"Still not ready to listen to truth or reason?" He shook his head. "So be it. But you better listen to me when I tell you this. Mother informed you Xandora's behind this, and I'm telling you it's her last hurrah. She's willing to fight to the death to get what she wants. And she's willing to take out anything and anyone in the process."

"Including you?"

"Of course. Would you be sorry?"

"The only thing I'm sorry for is ever having believed in you."

For just a moment stunned hurt shown in his eyes. Then the amber gaze gleamed dangerously bright, and his near seven foot frame stiffened as if unspent anger sought an outlet.

"Just be aware. She has designs on this area and your mountain, and she's brought him here as her second in command. So far, in the interest of keeping the peace in camp, Thurax and I've been tiptoeing around one another, but it's only a matter of time. He'll want retribution, and if he gets wind of you, he'll make it his mission to finish what he started with both of us."

At the thought of Thurax coming for Malachi, her hate momentarily faltered. Even if they were at odds, she couldn't imagine a world without him.

"Your *partner* is coming," Malachi said. Sarcasm and resentment flavored that one word, as if only he had a right to make such a claim.

She spun around, but didn't see anyone. Moments later, Lance walked out of the shadows and strode their way.

"Everything okay here?"

She stepped away from Malachi. "Yes, everything's fine. Dr. Lance Lawson, this is Malachi—Black." She made up the last name, his real one gave her fits trying to pronounce it. "He's an acquaintance, from the old days." Her heart ached—an acquaintance, what a joke, he'd been her lover, her world.

The two males sized each other up. Lance appeared ready to go to the mat for her, brave but unknowingly foolish. Dr. Lawson could no doubt take down just about any human, but squaring off with a Fae/sorcerer would end badly for him.

"Good to meet you," Lance said, offering his hand in friendship.

Port all but hissed out her anger. Malachi had obviously cast a spell of comfort over Lance, otherwise why would he so easily reach out to a towering stranger dressed in black, emanating dark vibes.

"The call to mess is in ten," Lance informed her, shoving his hands in the pockets of his camo jacket.

"Great. I'm starving," she lied.

"Sure you're okay?" He peered more closely at her.

"You bet. I'll be there in a minute."

Lance nodded and strolled toward the house, indulging in one backward glance at the entity she had thought never to see again. She made to follow.

"We need to talk," Malachi said, making her hesitate.

"You need to talk. I'm good," she snapped.

Yet another lie. It seemed to be her M.O. tonight.

After seeing him just now, she didn't know how anything in her world would ever again be considered good. A flash of dejection skittered across his face then disappeared. Good. Let him hurt, let him suffer.

"Really, I gotta go." She walked backward as she spoke.

He followed, gaining ground, reaching out, holding her back. "Give me a chance to explain."

"Why? It's over between us."

"Is it?"

She flung up a mind-shield, determined to block him from reading her true thoughts. A crooked smile curved his mouth ever so slightly. She hadn't been quick enough.

"Until we meet again, love" he whispered, his breath warm against her cheek.

Bold and aggressive, he dared to capture her mouth with his, melting her body and resolve. The times they'd made love swirled through her mind, making her dizzy, making her reach for him when running the other direction would have been the smart thing to do.

The supper bell clanged, startling them both, breaking their physical hold on one another. But nothing could break the soul to soul connection she felt for Malachi.

\*\*\*\*

He watched her walk away. She hadn't been quick enough with the mind-shield, not that he couldn't break through it given a few more moments. She still loved him. And he adored her, and he swore by all that was holy—and unholy—he'd win her back.

As he prepared to conjure wings, a motion in the woods caught his attention, and he ambled in the same direction. Spotting an unusually large and very beautiful fox, he followed deeper into the woods.

When they were secluded, Mother Nature transformed from fox to woman. "Your promise to keep your distance didn't last long," she reprimanded.

"Portence deserves to know Thurax is here."

"Yes, I agree. I was about to inform her myself once I caught her on her own. But don't push your luck. If I could find you this easily, so can he. And you could lead him right to her. Contain your hormones. That's an order."

**\*\*\*\***

Not hungry for food, Portence lingered outside under the stars, staring up at the sky. How in Hades had her life come to this? She was about to fight in one of the most important battles of her life, the first major one side by side with her sisters. Yet battle tactics and strategies no longer occupied her thoughts. All she saw was his face. He'd looked more mature, thanks to a few laugh-lines, but his golden eyes could still mesmerize, and she'd thoroughly enjoyed his mouth tasting her, devouring her. Malachi's powers were stronger than ever. She could sense them. Port thought she had become stronger too, but her resistance had faltered.

The aching in her heart overshadowed confusion and anger, growing stronger, nearly bringing her to her knees. She'd gone a long, long time denying needs and desire, rejecting intimacy of any kind with any being. She'd blamed the defense mechanism on him, telling herself he had ruined her for anyone else. And in a way he had. The longings inside of her, screaming for freedom, were for him only. He was the chink in the stone wall protecting her heart. Now it crumbled, spilling out pent up pain gathered across time and galaxies. Since the trash planet, her hate had fueled determination, keeping her going strong. If she let that go what was left to protect her? She would give in to him, wanting the love that had brought the greatest joy she'd ever known.

"Frick, frick, frick," she hollered, shaking a fist in the air at the Fates, or whoever was in charge of screwing up Fae destinies.

As if in answer to her shout in the night, an animal howled off in the distance. Unable to suppress a smile, she turned and headed for the house. Wolves unofficially lived in Colorado, but she recognized that hungry male "voice", and it didn't belong to a wolf.

## Chapter Five

The rain started in the middle of the night, and was still going strong the next morning. Despite the weather, Lance loaded last minute supplies into the troop carrier.

He supposed the lizard-headed Reptiles wouldn't mind the water, but maybe the cold would slow them down. It might even snow. That's how things went in Colorado—twenty-four hours could take you from shoveling snow, heavy as wet sand, to desperately seeking shade, sunscreen, and a cool drink.

He visualized the medical camp. Setting up the portable hospital in the nearby valley had seemed like a good idea at the time, but it might prove to be a questionable choice if the rain didn't let up. They'd chosen the area because it offered shelter, access to a highway, and a nearby creek ensuring if not potable at least running water. However, the stream he once prized so highly could become a torrent.

Maybe Mother Nature could talk to Mother Earth and do something about the weather. He chuckled wondering if he would ever find such a thought commonplace. A few months ago, the very idea would have had him questioning his sanity. Besides, why be so anxious for clear skies. It would likely bring them closer to battle, and although perhaps inevitable, never a good thing.

"Hey partner, need some help?"

He turned to see Port sauntering his way, the downpour not hurrying her along.

"Sure. How are you today?"

"Right as this dang rain," she said, grabbing a box, and handing it to him.

"So is your tall and somewhat scary friend still here?"

"No. I doubt you'll be seeing him again."

"Why's that? The two of you obviously have a pretty strong connection if the pheromones hanging heavy in the air were any indication."

"We're just old acquaintances," she insisted.

"And I'm the Easter Bunny. I could always tell when my daughter was lying too."

"Well, it's a long story."

"I imagine it is. The best ones usually are."

"Here's the short version. He left me for dead on a trash planet. Now he says he can't live without me."

"Whoa. He didn't seem like someone who would do such a thing." Lance had no idea what a trash planet was, but it didn't sound good.

"No, I didn't think so either—until it happened. He says he can explain, but he's only half Fae so I only half trust him to tell the truth."

Yikes, this just kept getting more and more intriguing. "What's his other half?"

"Sorcerer."

"Well damn. And that's bad?"

"Haven't been around many, have you. They can be a tad arrogant, pushy, and demanding all wrapped in a cloak of mystery and magic."

"I take it his last name isn't really Black."

"No. But as far as I'm concerned the color fits his heart and soul."

"Things aren't always what they seem, Portence. And very good people, and I use the term all-encompassing, have been known to do incredibly bad things, for extremely good reasons. Might not make it right, but sometimes the why is important."

"Are you speaking from experience?"

"Just saying a warrior's profession must put one in extraordinary situations. I know as a soldier and a doctor, it has me."

"That doesn't mean you desert common sense, basic decency, and your partner."

"No. It doesn't." So, they'd been partners once. In what, he could only imagine, but this added another connection, and a big heap of emotion to the mix.

She stood tall, her back stiff, her anger apparent—a condition she seemed prone to of late. Obviously they were in love, or at least in lust. He should probably back off and not pry. But it amused him to see this side of her. She came across as so tough. Again, just like his daughter. Being a female oceanographer, he imagined his stubborn offspring had faced some of the same difficulties Port faced being a female soldier. Acting tough worked as a good shield, a safe perimeter, but was lonely in the long run.

"Don't you start lecturing me about personal relationships, and all the crapdoodle that goes along with it," she added.

"Hey, I'm your partner now, and I'm just trying to make sure your love-life is under control. Don't want it to interfere with your judgment while you're watching my back." Well that sounded pretty harsh, but maybe it's what she needed.

She relaxed her stance. "You don't have to worry. I'm not like him. I'll always be there for you."

The way she said it, he knew she meant it.

\*\*\*\*

They continued to work in silence. Dr. Lawson had a calming effect on Port. Because of his age and rank, and because she thought he actually gave a flying fig about her, she respected his opinions and advice. But when it came to Malachi, it was a whole different story, with its own set of rules, ones alien to Lance in more ways than one.

Seeing Malachi had shaken her to the core, demolishing the walls of indifference built with such care, and at such emotional expense. She had never stopped loving him. Not really. But if she let him back in and he betrayed her again, it would be her undoing. They could ship her off to the institution from which Xandora had escaped.

He *had* betrayed her. Right? After recovering from the trash planet ordeal, she'd run blindly away from him, across one universe after another. Yet, she really never gave him a chance to explain. Why had she run? Why hadn't he come to find her?

When they had been together, they'd never talked about the future, or marriage, or kids, or much of anything other than their assignments. They never planned for anything except how to survive the mission they were on, only looking forward to when they could spend more time in one another's arms.

Did he deserve another chance? Did *they* deserve another chance? Time would tell. Besides, she wasn't even sure how to contact him. Although if she called to him in great need, like when she'd been so ill, he would hear her. Well she wasn't about to cry wolf just to see him again. He was obviously working for Mother. Did it involve keeping Xandora satisfied? A stab to the heart of a new sort took her by surprise—jealousy.

She wanted to contact Mother, maybe grill and worm some info out of her as to why Malachi had never come to find her. But Mother had a lot on her mind. So far the Council had bidden Mother to defer to the Fates as far as the cosmic outcome of this war—always a grand irritation with their leader.

Over the years, many, many years, Mother and the Fates had been known to go at it hammer and tong, creating a power struggle rather than a corroborative effort when it came to running the Multiverse. The Fates were mired in ancient thinking, another obstacle, as Mother Nature enjoyed both the tried and true, and the new and fantastic. However, as far as Port was concerned, this was no way to run a war. It seemed fraught with personal campaigns, and people at odds who should be pulling together.

"That's the last of it for now," Dr. Lawson said, drawing the tarp down, and her thoughts back to the present. Securing the ties, he closed off the back of the vehicle. "Let's head in for breakfast."

"Sounds good." Surprisingly she felt hungry today.

At the ranch house they joined Bliss, Solace, Tanner, and Nate, and as they gathered around the huge table. Alfonso indulged them once again with his culinary skills.

"I think we should use this annoying wet weather to our advantage," Tanner said, helping himself to another homemade buttermilk biscuit before passing the basket.

"Can't wait to hear this," Solace joked.

"We've been trying to nail down an excuse to evacuate Colorado Springs. I say we predict severe flooding. In this case it isn't true, but it happened in these parts only a few years ago so I don't think it will sound too suspicious. And although it would be voluntary, most folks would readily comply. We should also include the town of Fountain in case the fighting spills over in their direction."

"I've a meeting today with the Governor," Lance reported. "We're to discuss plausible reasons for the recent troop movement in the area, and for why all the roads connected to Cheyenne Mountain have been closed. We've already selected one member of the local news team deemed reliable enough to use for disseminating whatever excuses we come up with. You're welcome to join me, Tanner, and we can add your idea to the agenda. We could use your input too, Nate."

"I'm available anytime," Nate offered.

"What are we, chopped kidneys?" Bliss put in. "Wouldn't you like some female input or viewpoints?"

"I think it's liver," Port corrected, "but she has a point."

"Nothing personal," Lance defended. "Just trying to make it look less like a parade, or like we're ganging up on our allies when decisions are made. Besides, as of three months ago, the person in charge of Peterson Air Force Base is U.S. Air Force General Lori Robinson, the first woman to command NORAD and North Com. I think your female warrior status will be well represented."

"Well, all right then." Port nodded, and crossed her arms over her chest.

"If there's no other concerns on who's going, let's review some strategy." Tanner pushed away from the table, and gained his feet. Since meals usually had them all gathered together at least once or twice a day, they'd set up a small secondary war room, known as the annex, near the dining area. "We know Xandora is amassing her troops on the far side of Cheyenne Mountain," he began, "and once the rain lets up we expect contact. We can't just go in and bomb the hell out of them because they purposely set up near the dam." He stabbed a finger at the map already marked with a big black X. "If damaged, it really will flood the town, with heavy casualties.

"Our intention is to hold the west ridge on our side of the valley protecting the area where Dr. Lawson is set up. Logic dictates the enemy will want to fight in said valley so they can spread out in full formation. But to reach the valley, they must negotiate a narrow geological passageway when leaving the protection of the canyon. But of course, logic may not be our best friend considering we're dealing with their bat-shit crazy leader."

"Do we know what weapons are on hand?" Bliss asked.

"Thanks to Nate's aerial recon from his glide-by, our photos indicate a limited amount of ground weapons only. But they're state of the art, HK416's, M27's, RPG's, and regular hand weapons including grenades. There were also a few tents big enough to conceal larger munitions.

"Xandora shouldn't have been able to bring grand

scale equipment through the portal," Port put in.

"Correct," Lance spoke up. "She would have had to appropriate them here, and according to my contacts no military weaponry has been reported missing, and no purchases have flagged with our black market informers."

"That's good news, at least," Tanner acknowledged. "And since Mother had the hijacked portal closed, Xandora is stuck with the number of troops she has Earth-side. She can, however, shuttle troops from the east and west coast to this area. If she does, it's going to mean more than two to one, their favor." Tanner fell silent, his gaze skimming across each of their faces. "Trained and ready as we are," he said, voice as serious as it comes, "fighting these Reptiles is going to be a bloody affair. Our best chance of cutting them down to size would be making contact when they're coming through the narrow, nuts to butt.

"What's nuts to butt?" Bliss asked.

"Army lingo for tight single line formation," Port explained. "For us it would be boobs to back." That elicited a few chuckles, and brought a smile to their faces easing some of the tension. Who said war strategy meetings couldn't be fun?

They fell silent. Why hadn't Tanner mentioned Thurax? He probably didn't know the mercenary monster existed. Should she say something? She only had Malachi's word he was here. She needed more reliable proof. But if Thurax really were here, she could only imagine what other surprises Xandora had shoved up her satin sleeves.

**** 

Xandora's petulant scream echoed across the land,

Gini Rifkin

and with satisfaction she saw even Thurax shudder in its wake.

The weather was grating on her nerves. She hated it, she hated it, she hated it. And just look at her hair— all frizz. Where had all this stupid humidity come from? And where was her drink.

"Malachi," she hollered.

"Yes, my dove."

Suddenly he was at her side, drink in hand. By the gods he was handsome, darkly so, dangerously so. She felt better when he was around, but lately he'd been absent more and more. Several days ago, he'd been gone for quite some time, and no one knew where he gotten to. It worried and annoyed her. Of course when you were dealing with a sorcerer, one had to tread lightly and possibly expect he might need private time for conjuring, or whatever the hell he did.

She accepted the drink he held out. A Cosmopolitan—how delightful. Taking a little sip, she sighed, and her mood lightened. She did so enjoy an alcoholic beverage, and had ever since the Nectar of the Gods Party eons ago. She took another sip, a generous one. This pretty pink concoction made her feel so…cosmopolitan. With a giggle at her own humor, she reached for Malachi.

"Finish your drink, love," he advised, shifting to stand at her back.

He gathered her hair to one side, draping it forward, letting it tumble to her waist. Then he massaged her neck and shoulders sending waves of desire shooting through her body.

Arching back against the chair, she couldn't suppress the groan of pleasure any more than she had been able to suppress her prior scream of frustration. She rarely edited her thoughts or behavior. After all, being the second woman ever created should earn her some perks.

Polishing off the drink, she threw the glass at the little wood stove in the corner of her room. Staring up at Malachi, and offering her best sultry smile, she lost herself to his uncommonly good looks. "Let's go make love. It's been so long, my darling."

Arms extended, a purr in her throat, she pleaded with her eyes. It seemed like forever since he'd taken her in the savagely wonderful way he had, leaving her breathless and satisfied. In fact, he hadn't touched her since the first time he'd gone missing without permission.

\*\*\*\*

Malachi forced his mouth into a semblance of a smile. It never reached his eyes.

No way was this happening, not now, and not ever again. Since he'd visited Port when she lay dying in the hospital, he'd managed to elude Xandora and her extremely healthy sexual appetite. And it hadn't been easy.

"I'm waiting," she snapped, the sharp edge to her voice giving proof of her annoyance.

He was waiting, too. Waiting for the potion he'd put in her drink to take effect.

The times he'd lain with Xandora, had been purely mechanical, the experience never touching his heart, or enriching his soul. Enough was enough. Deceiving wasn't in his nature, it compromised his principles. Mother could consider this aspect of his obligation fulfilled.

Although his love for Portence knew no bounds—duty had its limits.

Chapter Six

"Where's Port?" Bliss asked.

Entering the barn, she sauntered over to where Solace finished cleaning the stall for her assigned horse, Raven. The big mare, black as Solace's hair, liked to prance around and show off every chance she got. Had to love a lady who liked to strut her stuff.

"I don't know. I haven't seen her lately." Solace set the shovel aside, grabbed the wheelbarrow handles, and pushed it out the open door to the manure pile. "Not since breakfast, anyway. Her horse is gone. Weren't they in the outdoor arena?"

"I just came from there," Bliss said. "I didn't see anyone."

Bliss' horse, Rocket nickered for her attention. A sorrel gelding, he matched Bliss' red hair, and aptly named, he could run like the wind. She grabbed a handful of alfalfa pellets and a feed pan, and took the treat over to him. "Maybe we better saddle-up and see where she went." She scratched Rocket behind one ear as he munched away. "Since Noodge has been introduced to the horses, and knows not to eat them, we could take him along to help track her down."

"Sounds like a good idea. Something sure has been bothering her lately. Any idea what?

"I get the feeling it has something to do with the dream I captured for her, the one about being on the trash planet. I don't think she's having nightmares anymore, but it could still be affecting her somehow even though it happened in the past."

"If what happened to her back there is connected to what happened to her in the hospital, then it's very much in the present. I think this mysterious *guy* she's mentioned is not just on the planet, but is nearby."

They each grabbed a bridle and slipped them on their respective horse.

"I'm betting you're right, and she's gone to find him," Bliss said, as she worked at the buckle. "She says he means nothing to her, but I think the *lady doth protest too much.*"

"What?"

"She says she hates him, but she really loves him."

"Oh. Wow. Is that good news or bad?"

"Let's make sure it's good. I'd like nothing better than to see Port happy again."

"Should we alert Nate and Tanner we're leaving?" Solace asked, leading Raven closer to the tack room and saddles.

"I vote no." Bliss shook her head, following along with Rocket. "We've become too dependent on our partners. We still owe our first allegiance to The Fae Warriors Alpha Team, and to the Sisters of Anu."

"I agree. We're soldiers, we can handle a little recon mission."

\*\*\*\*

Port held onto Mouse's bridle, as they crept forward side by side. Since midmorning, the rain had reduced down to halfhearted fits and starts, but the dark clouds sliding off the mountains to the west promised more serious weather to come—and soon.

During the lull in the waterworks, fog wrapped the world in a false sense of security. It rose up off the land as if escaping Hades through unseen cracks. The element was a double edged sword, giving shelter to her enemy as well as cover to her and Mouse.

Watching her footing, Port chose their path. Gray and mystical as the fog, occasionally Mouse pulled or push, directing her toward better choices. She felt protected by his size and strength, and safe in his gentleness. Quite the rare and special feeling.

"Be quiet as your name," she whispered, and smiled when he bobbed his head in understanding.

In the few days they had been together, she'd come to love this big gelding. A good listener, he made her believe things would be okay. He never offered unasked for advice like her sisters, or excuses like Malachi. These fleeting moments they shared, gave her a sense of joy and companionship in what lately seemed a world possessing little promise of happiness.

They circled the valley, reaching the ridge on the east side, and altering course around a jumble of rock, she paused to listen. Based on their most recent data, there should be a mishmash of Rep-built structures in the canyon just beyond the rim of rocks. That meant navigating some rough terrain if she hoped to gather firsthand proof Thurax lived and was actually here.

A warrior, he'd be close to the frontlines, yet demanding to be housed properly like the military genius he took himself for. No tent or sleeping in the mud for him. What an arrogant monster. Unfortunately, he'd earned the arrogance because he was so good at his job—killing. Anytime, anyplace, any method, Thurax was for hire.

The last time they had crossed paths was long ago and far away. A time she tried hard to forget. For him to be here meant the nightmare could come alive again. For him to be here also meant the nightmare could be killed once and for all.

But she wasn't about to take Malachi's word as golden. She needed to see for herself.

Skirting off to the right, she made better progress conquering the incline. Near the top, she eased Mouse under a high arched outcropping. If she took him any higher, he'd be silhouetted against the sky. Even gray on gray could catch a sentry's eye.

"Stay put, my beauty," she ordered.

Placing a kiss on his velvety muzzle, she dropped to the ground, and G.I Joe'd her way closer. Her camo rain gear and black pleather jumpsuit protected her from the wet terrain. She hadn't known pleather existed until recently. She'd always rationalized using the hides left by the meat-eaters of the world wasn't a bad thing. But this new material removed all guilt, and the fabric still hugged her like a second skin.

At the top, she eased up slowly to peer down into the open space below.

Organized and relatively quiet, the camp took her by surprise. Xandora obviously had help setting it up. Wheedling and grifting her way across the Universe, coercing others to do her bidding, the woman had always sounded more concerned with personal gain and pleasures rather than military strategy.

Grabbing the binoculars hanging on a strap around her neck, she took a closer look-see. Rugged terrain surrounded the Rep camp, giving them three-sided protection from an infantry attack. Of course, the E.T.

squad could special-op down the incline, but even at night they would easily be picked off. The Reps had been stockpiling too, so siege tactics didn't seem to be a viable approach. Perhaps the canyon could work against them. Boxed in, it would at least keep them contained and prevent them from melting back into the surrounding landscape.

Again, she regretted bombing the crap out of them was off the table.

Scanning the area she spotted a rusted out carcass of an abandoned semi-trailer. Vegetation appeared to anchor it in place as it clung to an incline. Activity around the barracks seemed pretty subdued, and although strategically sound, their site was waterlogged.

The enemy in true Reptile form slogged around in ankle deep mud, which made her appreciate all the more staying at Nate's. In this damp and cold, she would have thought the lizard lowlifes would be moving slower, but no such luck.

Did Xandora bed down in the camp, too? Probably not and Malachi would most likely be wherever she was. Good, no sorcerer around to detect if she cloaked her image to go in for a closer look. And it might just come to that. The weather didn't encourage hunkering down here all day, and eventually someone was bound to miss her back at the ranch house.

Mouse gave a huff. He wasn't much on standing around idle either—unless it was in a nice warm stall. Dang he was a gorgeous animal. When his ears pricked forward, she shifted her gaze back to the little canyon. A door on the tractor trailer squawked opened, and a hulking form emerged. She shrunk back. Thurax. Malachi *had* been telling the truth.

The odds of the Army E.T. Squad winning kept getting worse. Thurax was worth twenty men. Just to look at him, seven feet tall, he seemed to be all muscle and brawn, but you'd be wrong to discount his intelligence. He was designed for fighting. In the parallel universe from which he came, the males on his planet had evolved to facilitate warfare. Thick plates of outer dermis covered the tops of their heads, shielding their noggins like body armor. And although she couldn't see his eyes from this distance, she remembered them on the ship-to-ship monitor as being black and soulless.

Entering the restricted space between universes required permission, but occasionally *things* made it through. Thurax had been one of those *things*, and she and Malachi had been sent to find him. How had he survived? All the Space Counter Intelligence follow-up intel indicated he died then and there, in a blast that sent shock waves across the Absolute Zone. If she had been so wrong about Thurax being dead, what else had she gotten wrong regarding that day?

"What's going on?"

At the sound of the voice, Port gasped and slid sideways in the mud. So intent on her mission and remembering, she hadn't heard Bliss and Solace as they crawled up behind her. Getting so wrapped up in the past could get her killed in the present.

Bliss eased to the ground at her side, placing a hand on her arm. "Something's wrong. You didn't hear us coming."

Her gaze cut sideways to where Mouse stood in seclusion. He hadn't warned her they were sneaking up. But it wasn't Mouse's fault she'd dropped her guard.

He recognized them, and knew she was safe, and he was smart enough to not cause a ruckus, possibly alerting their enemy.

"What are you guys doing here," she countered.

"You can't leave the compound unannounced and not think we wouldn't worry and follow," Solace commented.

"Did you tell anyone where you were going?" Port asked.

"No," Bliss admitted.

"So it's okay for you two, but not for me?"

"Knock it off," Solace ordered. "You know it's completely different. We were looking for you. What were *you* looking for?"

In answer to her question Port drew the strap over her head and handed the binocs to Solace.

"Take a gander for yourself."

"Holy Mother of Creation. Who in blazes is that guy?" Handing the field glasses off to Bliss, Solace turned onto her back, and slid down closer to Port.

"His name is Thurax. The bane of our existence when Malachi and I...traveled together."

"Traveled together. What's that mean?" Bliss pressed.

Port blew out a heavy sigh. Guess it was time to enlighten her sisters on some of her secret past. But not here.

"Let's head back to the ranch, and I'll tell you guys what's going on."

The rain began to patter down in earnest, backing her bid to get moving.

"I just came out to verify whether or not that psychopathic soldier-of-fortune was really here."

Chapter Seven

"Okay, spill." Solace handed out cups of hot tea, as they sat at the table in their cabin headquarters.

Port set hers aside, her fingertips tracing the scars and initials carved in the old wood as she wondered where to begin. Evidently, her training had been quite different from her sisters'. She wasn't sure why Mother had singled her out for undercover work, maybe between the three of them Mother knew she took being away from home and on her own better than the other two. Or maybe she knew working alone while defying the impossible was right up her alley.

"Did Mother offer either of you the opportunity for special training?" She asked, now clasping the hot mug of tea to warm her cold hands.

"All of it seemed pretty special to me," Bliss said.

"Yeah, what exactly do you mean by *special*," Solace pinned her down.

"Undercover work, special ops missions." The following stunned silence was an answer in itself. "I wasn't even a year in when she broached the subject, making it sound like an opportunity of a lifetime." When this didn't garner a reaction or response, she continued. "My regular training was accelerated after which I entered the Space Counter Intelligence program."

"You were SCI?" Solace nearly choked on her tea.

"Officially, I still am."

Another round of silence followed.

"That had something to do with you ending up on the trash planet," Bliss filled in the blanks. "I saw you there in your nightmare, the one I helped tame for you."

"Yes. I was assigned to the area for other reasons, but ended up on that orbiting nightmare."

"And the seven-foot goon we just saw put you there?" Anger seemed to replace Solace's confusion.

"No, but he was the reason we were in that the sector."

"And just who comprises this *we* you're talking about?" Bliss asked.

"Malachi. The sorcerer who gave me this." She rested her hand on her chest.

Touching the Eolh tattoo had become a habit, like reaching for a good luck charm, an automatic response to thinking about him or hearing his name. Suddenly she realized she no longer rued the mark. Knowing his hands put it there, it felt like touching him.

"I knew it," Bliss declared, nearly spilling her drink. "He's the one who saved your life."

"He was my partner. And *he's* the reason I was on Darrius V."

"You better start from the beginning," Solace said.

Port scrubbed her hands across her face trying to clear her mind, trying to bring back all the details while suppressing the horror.

"Okay, here goes. First of all, I don't really have permission to let you guys know everything about my past. Not my idea to keep it secret, just the nature of the beast. But under the circumstances, even though I'm still an agent, you'll be safer if you have some knowledge as it applies to what's happening now. But keep it on the down-low. You don't tell anyone, not even *your* partners. This belongs to the Fae world." Both sisters nodded their agreement.

"And secondly, before I recently ended up in the hospital, I hadn't seen Malachi in almost three years."

"Oh, Port." Bliss reached out and touched her hand in sympathy. "How could you stand to be separated?"

"At the time I was glad. I hated him, Bliss. And the separation wasn't my choice, or his either I suppose. Mother made the assignments, and as you know, you don't question Mother's decisions." She hadn't thought about it from Malachi's point of view. But still, if he really wanted to, he could have found her.

"At the time, when we were partners, an underground group of brainiacs constructed an unsecured portal to allow indiscriminate crossings between parallel Universes. Mother was horrified, then mad as a momma Yukla bear. Parallel universe hopping is still verboten, unless by her command or permission."

"Yikes." Solace sat up straighter. "Total havoc could ensue if alternate realities started intermingling."

"And another yikes," Bliss cut in, "for your Yukla bear reference. I saw one during winter camp maneuvers on Norse-guard 12," she rambled on, caught up in the memory. "She was magnificent, blue as the streaks in your hair, Port, and at least twelve feet tall. We only outran her because we were in souped-up snowcrafts and—"

"The point being," Port interrupted, wanting to get the telling of the story over and done, "the point being, Malachi and I were sent beyond all the Norse-guard planets—to the Absolute Zone. We were between Universes."

The shocked expression on the faces of her sisters didn't come as a surprise.

"But they call it the A Zone because all entities are absolutely forbidden to go there from either side," Solace said.

"Well, Mother is in charge of the Divide, and we work for Mother, so—"

"Did you find the gateway?" Bliss asked.

"Yes. Found it and closed it. But Thurax and several various entities had already gotten through. Outraged over being cut off from returning to his home planet, he came looking for revenge.

"We played hide and seek with him for eight days, and never saw another soul. When you're out there, *no man's land*, isn't just an expression. And if by some statistical improbability you do cross paths with anyone or anything, it will probably want to kill you."

"Holy Carina. How'd you get away." Bliss leaned forward in her chair.

Rehashing all this sent Port's anxiety level off the charts, but it was a little late now to turn back, and this finally felt like the right time to talk about it—purging the negative energy she lived with.

"Made for speed, our vessel was considerably smaller than Thurax's, and it lacked serious weaponry. It was old. We stole it out of necessity when escaping our previous mission. Knowing we needed reinforcements, we headed for our galaxy. We were closing in on our border when he found us.

"The first blaster-shot clipped our engine, cutting power to half. No chance now to out run him or put any useful distance between us. Going on defense, Malachi cast a protective shield around us which deflected Thurax's smaller weaponry, but it required tremendous energy and concentration from him to keep it in place. We took evasive action as best we could, and vulnerable as hell, limped toward Norse-guard 23 and help."

"Couldn't you radio for assistance?" Bliss wrung her hands as if she experienced the same panic Port had felt.

"We were completely alone as far as allies. We sent distress signals of course, and hoped Mother had been keeping an eye on us. But technically, no other manned vessels should be in the area. We knew if we died out there no one would ever be the wiser."

"I'd have been biting on a stick to keep from screaming with hysteria," Solace said.

"No you wouldn't. You'd do what needed to be done because you're a warrior, and you wouldn't let your partner down." Remembering what came next, Port took a deep breath and willed herself to continue.

"The second blaster-shot incapacitated us even more, knocking us off our course. One escape pod was damaged, the other leaking fuel. We either both stayed, or only one left. Malachi wanted me to leave, but I wouldn't. Then we detected a blip on our scope—the trash planet. If we could land there, then together we'd have a good chance of surviving until the next trash trawler arrived. With renewed hope we burned the last of our fuel tempering our freefall in that direction. We were close, so close, holding onto one another when the third blast hit."

She took a moment, asking for hidden memories to

make themselves known, but she still couldn't fill in the blank as to what had happened next.

"AND?" her sisters prodded in unison.

"I woke up on the Darrius V, inside the one viable escape pod, now crashed and useless. The artificial atmosphere was breathable, barely, so I crawled out of the wreckage. Dusk had fallen, and when I looked up, there was fire and debris scattered across the sky. Much more than would have been created by the destruction of our little traveler. I assumed Malachi had somehow destroyed Thurax and his ship. Apparently, Mother and Malachi thought he was gone for good too."

She gave a shiver, and Solace poured more tea in her cup.

"Cold and alone, I realized Malachi had used sorcery to get me in the pod. I was mad and afraid and grieving. How could the man I loved think I could survive on a trash planet? How could the man I loved survive out there alone in a broken down, out of fuel, out of air, piece of junk? Fortunately, I managed to stay alive until a trawler landed. It had been delayed a few days, but after it dumped the trash, I made it onboard. "

Again silence ruled, and she decided she'd said enough. But Bliss wanted more.

"Have you talked to him about what happened? It sounds like he was trying to do the right thing."

"The halls of Hades are hung with good intentions. How can he explain abandoning me? How can he explain going years without contacting me? I would have rather stayed with him, facing death together. That's what partners do."

Or did they? Just seeing Malachi the other night for those few moments had her questioning and doubting her logic and reasoning. Maybe rather than dying together, he thought sacrificing one life to save another took priority. Is that what he'd thought he was doing? If so, she'd been wrong all this time.

She gave a weary sigh, and the armor protecting her heart from the outside world seemed to disintegrate a little more. Was it finally time to take another chance on the love she missed so badly, and had never stopped craving. If she did give him another chance, it would have to be on her terms.

The door to their war-room cabin burst open, sending the three Fae Warriors to their feet.

Tanner came through the door first, with Nate and Lance on his heels.

"What's wrong?" Solace's words took a backseat to Tanner's

"Where the hell have you been?"

They'd been found out.

"It's my fault." Port stepped forward, taking the blame. "I was informed an old enemy may have joined the ranks of the Reptiles, and I wanted to see for myself if it were true. Solace and Bliss came to find me. I'm the reason we all ended up AWOL."

All three men appeared furious, or more precisely ready to explode with anger.

Dr. Lawson stepped forward, military straight and steely-eyed, meeting her nearly toe to toe. Since he was the highest ranking officer in the group, as well as being the oldest, she guessed he felt obligated to do the dressing down.

"You know better than to pull a stunt like that, Major." He barked out the words like a drill sergeant. "Yes, sir," she hollered back, not missing a beat, or the little gasps of surprise from Bliss and Solace. Darn, no more keeping her rank a secret.

"You endangered yourself, and those who came to find you." Lance took two steps back, his expression not easing up one bit. "Report," he demanded, arms folded across his chest.

"The enemy camp appeared quiet, sir. With pockets of shouting and shoving. They're knee-deep in water so I imagine even Reptiles can get tired of being wet. They have stockpiles of fuel and weapons."

Bliss stepped up to stand on her right. "They have an old tractor trailer," she reported. "We saw the enemy Port was talking about coming out of said makeshift housing, sir."

All three males turned their attention to Bliss, and when they relaxed their shoulders in unison, Port knew Bliss had applied her ability to compel on them—good one, sis. No use everyone getting mad and huffy about a little personal reconnaissance. Nothing bad had come of it, and in fact, they'd gleaned a bit of new information.

"He's a mean-looking, green-haired brute," Solace said, taking up position on the left. "And he appears to have his own little entourage."

The Sisters of Anu stood tall, the bond between them never stronger. Port reveled in the surge of energy, and she swore each man leaned backward—just a smidge—but enough to tell her the combined power of the Fae Warriors remained fearsome, as well as awesome.

"Well, just see it doesn't happen again," Nate said, offering up his share of anger and worry. "While you're at my place I'm responsible for you." He added the last as if in the face of their united front he better come up with a reason for his dictatorial attitude.

"We'll keep it in mind," Port promised. "Now go away."

The men didn't move, and the sisters, in unison, put their hands on their hips, strengthening their position. Port felt their collective energy jump another notch.

Tanner opened his mouth, then closed it.

Lance shook his head.

Nate manned the door, and they left.

**\*\*\*\***

"Dang, pretty impressive, eh," Nate said, when they were outside with the door tightly closed at their backs.

"Glad they're on our side," Tanner put in. "Did you ever notice," he added, glancing at the other two, "when they're all in the same room, the air smells like flowers?"

Nate nodded. "Boy I'm glad you said that. I thought it was just me, and I was having an attack of phantosmia."

"Ah, yes," Dr. Lawson clarified, "a condition where one smells phantom scents. I picked up on it too. All I know is these three blossoms are all too real, and they come with thorns."

## Chapter Eight

Malachi sat and watched it rain.

His *familiar*, a red-tailed hawk, took shelter in a nearby cottonwood tree. He'd been using his companion to keep an eye-in-the-sky on Portence, and knew she had ridden out toward the camp. At least now, if she didn't believe anything else he told her, she would believe him regarding Thurax.

The thought of slipping away to meet up with his beautiful Fae put his guts in a knot. The temptation plaguing him night and day. But her sisters always seemed to be nearby, and he wanted her all to himself. Besides, he truly meant to keep the remainder of his promise to Mother. After all, she had saved his life, but without his true love, living had become an exercise in futility and loneliness.

With a sigh, he stretched out his legs, and crossed them at the ankles. Leisure intervals, although rare, had become his enemy. He usually spent them thinking about Portence, reliving their time together. It was all he had since she kept denying him the making of new memories.

How odd he, Portence, and Thurax should all end up together on the side of this rocky mountain, light years away from where it all started. At least now he could take his time and enjoy planning what he'd like to do to the marauding mercenary. The first time they'd been on a collision course, leaving only moments to think and act. The results hadn't been what he'd hoped for, but he'd risk the consequences again if it meant saving Portence.

While drifting in the Absolute Zone, Thurax's third attack had knocked Portence unconscious, and the growing lack of oxygen began to take its toll on his own ability to function. He'd spotted Darius V just over the line, back in their Universe. It he could get Portence safely there, she could hitch a ride off the planet with the trash trawler on course and heading the same way. What could go wrong? It had been a decent plan, but what followed had been beyond his control.

After sending Portence on her way in the more operational of the two emergency pods, he'd manipulated the fuel crystals on their main ship so they would overheat and implode. Setting their craft on a crash-course for Thurax's, he'd sealed himself in the other broken down escape vehicle, and jettisoned away from the soon to be exploding vessel.

But sorcery in No Man's Land required phenomenal energy, and he soon realize he'd traded one dire situation for another.

Their ship exploded prior to reaching Thurax. Not a direct hit, but the ricocheting debris wreaked serious damage. The blowback, however, sent him hurtling through space, his escape pod out of control, his brain out of bright ideas, and his heart out of hope of ever seeing Portence again.

What he hadn't known until later was part of Thurax's ship had torn loose, and hurtling through space, it slammed into the trash trawler. Thinking the ship was under attack, the computer driven craft went into defense mode and fired back. A battle ensued resulting in Thurax's ship exploding in a magnificent ball of fire. It seemed impossible for anyone or anything to survive the inferno, but somehow he had. The trawler had taken a hit as well, leaving it in deep-space trouble. It lost power for two days, stranding the only woman he'd ever loved on one of the worst planets in any galaxy.

Unaware until later of this chain of events, and powerless to do anything had he known, Malachi rode the solitary tin can drifting deeper into the land of limbo and farther away from the trawler and the trash planet. As the oxygen dwindled lower and lower, he sent out one last distress signal then went into hibernation mode, not sorcerer's magic, just a sorcerer's inherent skill.

According to Mother, he'd come as near to dying as had Portence. For three months the escape pod wobbled through space, eventually leaving the Multiverse dead zone where he fortuitously crossed paths with a transport barge. After his rescue, Mother sent him home to Mystica where it took another three months to recover.

She'd apologized for not finding him sooner, but the Multiverse was a large place and she'd been busy elsewhere. He and Portence were not her only operatives, but they'd been on one of her most dangerous missions.

Learning Portence, whom he loved and cherished more than he ever thought possible, had made it out alive came as a great relief. But relief turned to grief when he learned she hated him. He wanted to explain, but wasn't given the chance. Mother said she refused to see him, and then he'd been assigned to Crystalline B—

the ice planet where crystals were mined in the frost fields. He didn't mind the cold, for his heart felt frozen anyway.

With Portence always on his mind, he grudgingly followed orders, and nearly two years later Mother reassigned him to track down Xandora. The silly female had led them all a merry time-consuming, chase. And now he was here.

An abomination of womanhood, Xandora took everything deemed holy about being a female, and turned it into dominating evil. Their running into one another and becoming *friends,* had been a planned coincident, and he hadn't needed magic to breech her walls, personal or otherwise. Mother called it taking one for the team. Unfortunately, Mother still saw redeeming qualities in Xandora which totally escaped his observations. Perhaps he was too close to the problem to see it clearly.

He didn't really give a damn about this war, or trying to keep Xandora alive. Truly his heart wasn't into either assignment anymore. Did that make him sound like a cruel bastard? He wasn't sure he cared. All he wanted, all he could think about, was Portence.

When the rain stopped, he gained his feet and stepped down onto the grass. The image-projection of a cozy porch he'd been sitting upon dissolved away leaving a chair teetering on a board supported by cinderblocks. He'd created the scene for his own amusement. Maintaining the false reality in place for Xandora, however, was not amusing. It took time and concentration, and tedious monitoring. Of course, she cared nothing for what befell anyone around her.

She would have him creating a castle with all the

trimmings if he hadn't told her using so much power would leave him at a disadvantage should protecting her require his magic. With self-preservation ranking at the top of her priority list, she'd bought the fib. Lying didn't come easily to him, but looking out for himself came high on his list too. He had better things to do with his time, like mending fences rather than creating them, and watching Thurax was crucial.

A master at warfare, the chartreuse marvel of muscle practiced his skills daily, exhibiting feats of strength which impressed the Rep soldiers. He was the only reason the Reps showed any discipline at all. And he was also the reason why those who rebelled were soundly and quickly punished, usually with a whip.

Malachi had quickly decided that Thurax knowing he was here was a good thing. It would keep his interest and eyes focused in this direction—away from Portence. So far he didn't think Thurax knew she was nearby.

Obviously, she could take care of herself, but to protect her was a natural and primal instinct in him. No matter what she said, she belonged to him, and he always looked after his own.

****

Xandora exhaled long and hard, and with a conscious effort, relaxed the scowl twisting across her face. Angry expressions left wrinkles—no use marring her beauty on top of everything else. But who knew taking over a planet would be this complicated. The humans were smarter and better equipped than she had been lead to believe. Again she had been deceived by the male of the species. From Apollo to Zeus, they never took her seriously. All her life, people had lied to her while kowtowing to her stupid sister. Now it was her turn to shine. And if she couldn't take over this orbiting paradise, the achievement a testament to her brilliance, she'd darn well blow it up. That would get everybody's attention. Either way, it would go viral on Spacebook, and she'd be famous.

The computer in her makeshift office finished calculating, and now spewed out data from each outlying camp. All across the globe her troops were creating chaos, but due to lack of numbers, they were reduced to hit and run attacks. And thanks to uncaring MoNat she couldn't bring any more Reps in from the outer realms. Even her own Mother was working against her. Uniting her troops seemed the obvious answer to Xandora's problem. She would bring the majority of her earthbound personnel here.

Unfortunately, the gathering would take time. Meanwhile, she must hold the territory she'd already eked out here, disgusting and uncouth as the surroundings were. Thank the gods, Malachi masked the horrible conditions in which she found herself.

And speaking of Malachi, where was he? She needed her Malachi. The wall on her right had started to deteriorate. She didn't want to see the Reptiles out there slogging around in the mud. Just because they were her soldiers, it didn't mean she must be forced to gaze upon the scaly dirty beasts.

Grabbing her handheld she punched in the preprogramed number. It went directly to Malachi, and meant she needed him immediately. She refused to be left alone in this quagmire.

"Malachi," she screamed. "Malachi, where are you, dammit?"

"Calm yourself, Xandora. I'm right here."

"Oh, I didn't hear you coming."

"No, how could you?"

"What? Never mind. And I can darn well be uncalm if I want to. Becoming the global leader of this planet is taking too long. I've devised a new strategy. An influx of personnel will be reporting to this area. I'm taking over the mountain, along with as many civilian hostages as possible. We can barter the humans to force Mother to open the portal so more of my Rep soldiers can come through."

"And then what?" Malachi asked.

"Then we take over the planet, with our command center here."

"Once the general public realizes what is going on, you'll have more to contend with than just the E.T. Squad, Xandora. The Earthlings may panic at first, but then they'll fight back. Every man, woman, and child will be shooting at us. The humans are allowed to carry weapons, and they know how to use them."

Aaarrr. She leaped to her feet and glared at him.

"My orders have gone out," she snapped, "and I'm not changing them now. You are so pessimistic and disagreeable of late. Not supportive of my cause at all. You can be replaced, you know. There are dozens of entities out there who would deem it an honor to worship me."

"No doubt there are, Xandora. But it's a little late in the game to vet another sorcerer. And I promise, you won't care for me as an enemy."

Her spine stiffened at the warning. Malachi had become rebellious and inattentive of late, and now he dared to threaten her. A retort clamored for release, but the fire in his amber eyes scared her silent. She took a step back, checking her anger. Sometimes she forgot the extent of his abilities. She must remember not only what he could do *for* her, but *to* her.

"I'm sorry, darling," she conceded, striking a provocative pose, recalling too late sorcerers were less affected by the charms she'd garnered at great expense. Pandora had gotten all her life-gifts for free, of course. Another offense to add to the list. Then again, Malachi was a crossbreed, only half sorcerer and not immortal. Besides, come the day he wouldn't bend to her will, she always had Thurax.

She recalled the night Malachi discovered the glorious rogue beast numbered among her ranks. His reaction had nearly frightened her into a fainting spell. The revelation had come to light over dinner, and he'd been furious. She swore storm clouds, complete with lightning and thunder, had swirled around the dining room, a physical apparition of his anger. At the time, Malachi made her promise not to alert the green-haired warrior of his presence.

Then a mere few days later, he told her never mind, and that he'd made sure the alien warrior knew he was here. That irked her to no end. Now she couldn't lord the information over him for personal gain. He'd become very unpredictable, and day by day less accommodating. He seemed to forget who led this invasion.

Let's see how he liked this next bit of news.

"After the majority of my men have arrived," she said, nonchalantly, "I think blowing up the dam would be a nice diversion. We'll see how the humans enjoy swimming for their lives."

Malachi turned and stared at her. Now he was paying attention to her.

Chapter Nine

"I still think using the weather to our advantage is the best option," Tanner stated. "Like I mentioned before, a few years ago, this area suffered flooding of near Biblical proportions. With the previous disaster fresh in their minds, the civilians won't think twice if told to evacuate the town for similar circumstances." He paused and glanced out the window. "To be honest, if the rain continues at this rate, in conjunction with the erosion from recent wildfires, the runoff could be pretty bad. Anybody got a better idea for relocating the "town folk" to safety."

Port shook her head along with everyone else, her gaze scanning the war room cabin. It was starting to feel familiar. One of Bliss' totes hung on a wall peg, someone had brought in a pillow for the chair by the window, and personal coffee mugs were lined up on the counter. They were a family unit as well as a military one—it might not be protocol, but it was nice.

When the room remained silent and business seemed at an end, Dr. Lawson gained his feet. "Unless you need me as a liaison in town," he said, "I'm heading back to the field hospital. My darn portable MRI is on the fritz. Thing's brand new. Still got the old fashion x-ray machine, though. We'll get by."

After Tanner gave a nod of dismissal, and Nate made a promise to help if so requested, Lance headed for the raingear hanging near the door.

Port scrambled to her feet and followed. Sometimes, it seemed odd they were assigned partners. Their skills were so diversified it seemed to keep them apart more than draw them together.

"Watch your back out there," she said, as he shrugged into his outerwear. "You're nearly as close to the enemy territory as our perimeter guard, and I don't think those flippin' red crosses on your tents and equipment will save your ass if things go FUBAR."

"Nice talk, young lady," he chided. Then he grinned. "But partner to partner, I appreciate the sentiment, and not to worry. We have a few non-medical pieces of equipment—or more correctly pieces of equipment the Army doesn't know we appropriated. We're compassionate, not stupid. You watch your back, too."

He trudged out the door, through the rain, and climbed into the jeep. Then with a thumbs up, he headed out.

She joined her two sisters who had volunteered to accompany Tanner in getting the evacuation process started. Right now, he was on the phone with an employee he knew from working undercover at NOAA. That was when the Reptiles had first landed on Earth. It seemed like eons ago, but had only been a little over a month.

Tanner needed his buddy to broadcast erroneous flood warnings and weather alerts. At first, the guy resisted. If he got caught it would mean his job or worse. But when Tanner explained they were tracking down the group involved in the death of their mutual friend, Ralphie, it was a no brainer.

Gini Rifkin

By the time they reached town, the weather bulletins were already flying across the airways. The legitimate sounding information had the Mayor quickly believing their tale of impending doom, and he began issuing orders to the Chief of police. Two nearby towns were harder to convince requiring a call from the Governor who'd been prepared beforehand. There was nothing left to do now but wait.

"Well things certainly went better than I expected," Tanner said. "I guess we may as well go back to Nate's." They piled into the gas guzzling Hummer—a nice piece of equipment, if you could keep it properly fed.

Rather than heading straight out, they took the long way around giving them a chance to scout out the town, and get a sense of the layout. If things didn't go smoothly, they could be called back to help with the evac. And once the fighting started, it could spill over in any direction, and the Reps might find the resources offered by the abandoned city appealing.

Sitting in the back of the vehicle, beside Bliss, Port stared out the side window—barely seeing the shops and houses as their images flashed by. Then a raven sitting on a lamp post caught her attention. The creature's brilliant black feathers reminded her of Malachi's black hair. Again her thoughts locked onto her ex-partner. Everyone else seemed convinced his actions had been in good faith, done only with virtuous intent. And although she'd finally decided to give him a chance to explain, part of her doubted she would be swayed by anything he could say. Another part desperately depended on it.

"Hey," Bliss said, nudging her with her elbow.

"How you doing, sis?""

Since it was too hard to hide her emotions from Bliss and her empath abilities, she supposed she might as well give telling the truth a try. "If I ever see him again, I'll listen to whatever lame excuse he's come up with."

Bliss grabbed her arm and squeezed enthusiastically. "I'm so glad to hear you say that."

Guess she didn't need to explain who the *he* was to whom she referred, apparently she and Malachi were linked as a couple. "Well don't get too excited," Port warned. "With the whole Reptile situation about to bust wide open, it could be some time before we're face to face again, if ever."

"Well you never know."

"Ain't it the truth. About so many things."

"The two of you belong together. I can feel it. It's my job," Bliss added.

"I don't want to belong to anyone."

"Yes, you do—so much so it scares you. It's a leap of faith, Port, like the first time you jump off something really, really high—I mean you're-gonna-die-if-this-doesn't-work high. Remember? Mid-fall you conjure wings and there's a little pause when you don't know if it'll work. And even if it does, will it be in time to save you. Your heart seems to stop, you can't breathe, your mind is blank, yet filled with too many thoughts to comprehend. Then suddenly you're flying and not falling, laughing like never before—you did it, you're alive."

"I remember that moment, vividly," Port said, with a laugh and rush of adrenalin. "And your point is?"

"Take the leap, he'll be your wings. Then you can

soar together."

*Soar together*. Head back against the seat, Port closed her eyes. If Bliss only knew what memories her words unleashed. Her heart ached for Malachi. Her body longed for him. But her mind still warned he was dangerous.

**** 

Since the city evacuation worked on a voluntary basis, it meant completion of the process could take a few days, and might leave the most stubborn of civilians in place and in jeopardy.

Bliss understood their reasoning. It was hard to leave one's home even in the best of circumstance. It also meant the Fae Warriors and E.T. Squad would make no attempt to engage the enemy until given the all clear. In the meantime, it created an opportunity for Bliss to find Port's one and only. She had to figure out a way to get them together.

To put her plan into action, she lied to Solace and Port, telling them Nate had asked her to help work on the portable rechargers. Then she told Nate she'd be busy with her sisters checking equipment and working out. Tanner had Noodge brushing up on sniffing out bombs, so no one should miss her. And although she wished her furry baby was doing something less dangerous, her plan sounded foolproof.

Cloaking her image, Bliss took to the air. The rain made obfuscation a little tricky, but if one kept moving, it worked fairly well. It just had to. She needed to make Port happy again. Going into battle with a wounded soul created bad energy. One moment of lost concentration could mean death. Besides, matchmaking was so much fun.

Mother had aligned Malachi with Xandora—a logical move, offering her a spy directly in touch with the Queen of the Reptiles and her plans. But Bliss got the impression Xandora pulled the strings from afar. She wouldn't be in dirty, noisy, camp central. As she gazed down into the canyon, she noticed a house on the hill. Although rundown, it seemed like a good place for the demented demi-goddess. Would Malachi be there too?

Hovering, Bliss closed her eyes, mentally searching for signs of magic. If she could zero in on him when he was alone, she could avoid crossing paths with her Nasty Nibs. What was that? Her eyes snapped open. There were two fields of supernatural power. The enchantment over the house felt pure. The energy by the semi-trailer felt dark and muddled. She swooped in closer to the latter.

Did a sorcerer other than Malachi hold sway over the area? The vibrations were noxious and unwholesome, and they had to be coming from another wizard, warlock, enchanter, magus—good grief, who knew what dangerous creature had been hired or coerced into joining the fray. But if she had detected the other spell-caster, surely Malachi and Mother would know of this dark presence as well. Unless he'd just arrived.

As she pondered, an altercation broke out between two Reps. No big surprise there. Patiently waiting for new orders and playing nice would be out of character for these scaly brutes. Besides, minor scuffles and skullduggery often surrounded war camps, with members on every level fighting for power in the hierarchy. Thurax seemed especially unlikely to just sit around whittling while waiting for action. She'd bet her entire stash of Monopoly money the bad mystic vibes had something to do with him. This bore further investigation.

Landing near a vent on the roof of the trailer, she dropped wings, leaned in close, and pointy Fae ears on high alert, she listened hard.

"It's about time you got here."

"You risked much in sending for me, Thurax. And I have risked much in coming."

"We'll both be well paid, Gorlock. You in money and I in revenge."

Malevolence of a grand nature filled Thurax's voice, each word ground out with palpable hatred.

"Are you sure I'm safe and they don't know I'm here?" Gorlock questioned.

His voice, smooth as rancid oil, made him sound like a used sandblaster salesman. He also sounded frightened, but of whom, Mother, Xandora, or Malachi?

"Half-wizard or whole, Malachi will detect you eventually. Then he'll be our biggest threat. On the bright side, her majesty, the bitch, barely knows what's going on in her own head. And while she and her magic man keep company at a distance, I've organized the Reptiles. When the time comes, they'll answer to me, not her. She tries to rule by tantrum and idle threats. I rule by fear. Fear always wins."

Bliss almost felt a sorry for Xandora, the silly female. She thought to conquer a world, yet couldn't control her own men, while enemies within planned a takeover. But enough eavesdropping. She needed to get airborne and find Malachi. As she stood, she accidentally kicked loose the rusted flange around the vent. Metal on metal, it clattered across the top and over the edge, loudly landing on a pile of junk.

"What the—" The voice inside fell silent, and heavy footsteps followed.

Thurax bolted out the back door. For a large forbidding figure, he moved quickly, circling the lopsided semi-trailer upon which she huddled.

Bliss conjured wings, the process difficult while maintaining her cloaking devise in the rain. Something was wrong. As she leaped into the air, she slipped on the rain slick surface and fell to her hands and knees. She felt trapped in triple gravity unable to lift off. Her cloaking devise faded, and gazing over the side, she came face to face with Thurax. He stood staring up at her. The man at his back, waving his wand around and uttering incantations, had to be Gorlock.

There went her grand plan.

Unable to fight the dark magic, and seeing no alternative, she eighty-sixed her useless wings, and ran across the metal roof. Leaping onto the top of a nearby military vehicle, she scrambled over the side, and hit the ground running. What was she going to do? She couldn't out run them all the way back to the ranch. She started to call out to her sisters, and then thought better of it. She would be drawing them into a dangerous situation. One they would jump into for emotional reasons, not reasons based on military logic.

Dodging a stockpile of fuel drums she juked to the right, slid in the mud around a boulder, and smacked full-bore into the biggest, most gnarly, Reptile she'd ever seen. Sturdy as the rock she'd just avoided, she bounced off of him. Not going down without a fight, she took a defensive stand.

A noise at her back had her turning in time to see the cargo net hovering in the air. Unable to avoid the trap, she dropped to the ground and covered her head with her arms, protecting herself as the metal reinforced mesh crushed down on her. She kicked and clawed to no avail, then retrieving her KA-BAR knife, she sawed at the thick unyielding strands. A painful kick to the ribs halted her actions.

"What have we here?" It was Thurax's voice, and it had been his foot plowing into her side.

"Want me to kill her?" The excitement accompanying the words was more frightening than the words themselves. She shifted her gaze to the Rep she'd run into. Saliva dripped from his mouth, and his eyes shone bright with anticipation. He wore a ragtag shirt with badges and fruit-salad, indicating a high ranking officer. The name Botu was written above the pocket.

"I hardly think such immutable action necessary," Gorlock said, joining her tormentors. Tall and reed thin, as if drained of all humanity, he leaned closer. His mouth twisted into a vicious smile. The smell roiling off of him seemed a mixture of body odor and strong herbs. "It would be more fun to play with her for a while."

"You won't touch her unless I say so," Thurax growled, towering over both of them.

The alien warrior, dressed in a leather vest and cross-gartered pants, could have stepped off the cover of the ancient Beowulf manuscript, one of her favorite bits of literature—until now.

"Restrain her and bring her to me." Turning he strode back to the semi-trailer, his long legs eating up the distance in record time.

Gorlock motioned several Reps closer. They lifted the net and reached for her.

Chapter Ten

"Whoa Noodge, hold on buddy. What's the matter?" Solace tightened her grip on the leash and leaned backward, using her body as a counterweight in hopes of slowing the critter down.

"Hey, babe, let me help." Tanner hurried over, and wrapping his arms around her from behind, he grabbed hold of the leash as well.

Upset, the Rapran dug in with his claws and gaining purchase, towed the two of them across the hardwood floor of the dining room of the main house.

"What the heck is the matter with him?" Tanner asked, his warm breath tickling the back of her neck. "He seemed fine when we were working on bomb sniffing."

Solace wished the crazy hairball would give up the fight so she could enjoy being cozied by her partner. "I don't know," she answered over her shoulder. "Port went to find Bliss. Maybe she can calm him down. I've never seen him like this."

Port returned at a run, and out of breath. "I can't find her."

"Maybe she went for a ride," Solace suggested, making no progress with the big critter that had become one of the family.

"Nope, Rocket's still in the barn. Nate hasn't seen her either. Easy Noodge, we'll find her." Port stepped in front of the Rapran trying to head him off.

"She must be in trouble," Tanner said. "It would explain why Noodge's so upset."

"That's an idea I don't even want to contemplate, but one we can't afford to ignore," Solace agreed.

"We could turn him loose and follow him?" Port suggested.

"I don't think we have much choice." Solace's grip began to slip.

"I'll round up some of my men," Tanner volunteered. "You two follow Noodge."

****

Malachi hadn't been able to reach Mother Nature, and the situation here was growing worse in leaps and bounds.

More soldiers showed up by the hour, and auxiliary creatures popped up out of nowhere. This led to fights breaking out on a regular basis because of too many Reps in too small a space. The mountainside camp felt like a volcano ready to erupt. And now dark magic was being used—Gorlock was here. He'd felt him the moment he arrived.

They'd tangled years before while training on the planet Mystica. Even back then Gorlock leaned toward the dark side. Now he used his run-of-the-mill powers for true evil. Malachi believed their gifts should be used for good, to do otherwise constituted an effrontery, a sacrilege to the wise arts. Gorlock also resented the fact Malachi, a Fae/sorcerer crossbreed, had been granted such training and power in the first place.

Giving up on reaching Mother, yet honoring his word to ferret out information for her, Malachi slumped down onto the chair in the hallway. In the nearby room,

Xandora grilled a Reptile newly arrived from another part of the country. She rarely spoke to, or looked upon, any of the Reptiles unless he glammed them. Today she insisted her commander look like a medieval knight. The woman was delusional—and dangerous.

Following a great roar of anger, the Rep who had been in conference stomped out of the room. Malachi let the illusion fade from the beast while he maintained it around the shabby domicile. Xandora slammed the door shut nearly catching the departing soldier's tail.

A few heart beats later, Malachi followed the commander from the house, and cloaking his image, he meandered outside unseen. What he felt next stopped him cold, and changed his plans of following the Rep.

He sensed rather than heard the scream. There was a Fae nearby. He concentrated. Not Portence. One of her sisters then. And Gorlock was stirring again, flexing his feeble mental muscles. His spells spelled trouble.

Ignoring thoughts of caution, he tracked the energy source. Being nearly a level ten, he should be able to hide his approach from Gorlock—that little weasel was barely a six. The vibrations grew stronger as he reached the rusted out tractor trailer. No big surprise there. Thurax and Gorlock were made for one another, and what better place for two villains to hang out and cook up their plans for battle glory. Their combined power and evilness could be formidable.

The Fae energy he felt was in there as well. That *did* come as a surprise, and not a good one. Circling around to the far side, he peeked through the wall where the rust had created a handy peephole. What he saw had him biting back an expletive.

Seeing a facsimile of the face he loved framed in

red hair rather than white, gave him pause. It was Bliss. When he and Portence had been partners, she often spoke fondly of her sisters, regaling him with stories of their youthful antics. He almost felt he knew them, making what he now witnessed even more hurtful. A livid bruise on Bliss' left check, marred the familiar features, and her bound hands were attached to a rope and pulled up over her head. Her expression remained fierce. In fact, if looks could kill, Thurax and Gorlock would be dead. Over all, she didn't look too worse for wear—yet.

Following his instinct to rush in and rescue her, Malachi's headed for the door. Then he checked the movement and forced himself to more rational thinking. He would welcome a personal battle with the green-haired beast and his charlatan of a necromancer, but it could also incite the ready-to-boil-over war for which the Reptiles were definitely itching.

Maybe he could send the entire semi-trailer rolling down the hill. It would look like an accident, but Bliss would be injured too. He had to think of something.

****

Dismounting, Solace and Port unloaded the gear they'd brought along.

"Stay put," Solace ordered Noodge.

Before they left the ranch, Alfonso had privately spoken to the critter. The wonderfully curious man had an uncanny connection to horses, and apparently to Raprans. *"Until he is with her again, he will obey you,"* he'd told Solace, and thank goodness, his words had proven correct.

"Except for the rabble over yonder, it's quiet as the backside of the Moon here," Solace said, glancing around.

"Yeah," Port agreed. "Any indigenous animal with half a brain has already left the area."

The horses snorted and rolled their eyes. They'd been brave in the face of what they could smell coming, but at this point their terrified condition would probably be more liability than asset. "I guess we might as well turn the horses loose. They should get out of here too, and they know the way home."

Making sure they couldn't step on the reins, they sent them packing. Then they scrambled the rest of the way to the top of the ridge, Noodge at their side.

Port raised her head first trying to get a bead on the enemy. "Holy craptoid."

Solace popped up on her left. "Gees, the buggers don't look all that well armed, but there's sure a whole lot more of 'em than the last time we had a peek."

Noodge lay at her side, issuing a pitiful whine with tears in his eyes. She hugged him. "We'll find her," she reassured the Raptan once more.

Although hampered by the canyon walls, the surprisingly well-organized horde, in full Rep mode, preformed maneuvers. Grabbing the binoculars hanging around her neck, Solace studied them more closely. They wore camo cargo pants and heavy boots, and a few carried serious weaponry. But from the belt up, they were unclothed, and the shiny scales on their muscular bodies and bobbing heads reflected the gloomy daylight in a most menacing way. Like a glistening sea, they closed ranks and washed back and forth over the rugged terrain.

Nose in the air, catching their scent, Noodge growled and went into guard mode.

"As far as the lay of the land, we have the height advantage," Solace said, trying to bolster her own spirits as well as her sister's.

"So did King Harold against William the Conqueror, and you know how that turned out," Port countered. "Bliss is in there somewhere or Noodge wouldn't have led us here, but I wish I knew exactly where."

"Why in the Multiverse would she come here in the first place?" Solace lowered the field glasses, and used her own hypervision. "And why can't we feel her, or connect with her." Not many good answers came to mind for those questions. "There were no signs of a skirmish or intruder at the ranch. She must have left of her own free will."

"Guess we won't know until we find her—and give her a piece of our minds for scaring the stuffing out of us," Port threatened. "Now I know why Tanner, Nate, and Lance were so mad when they couldn't find us."

"Speaking of Tanner." Solace retrieved her hand held and gave him a call.

She updated him on their whereabouts, and insisted Bliss was in the enemy camp. He told her Nate had no idea why Bliss had gone missing, or why she would go there. They spoke a few minutes longer, then she heard gunfire on Tanner's end. He wouldn't be coming to help anytime soon.

"Bad news," she said to Port. "A splinter group of Reps is heading for Colorado Springs, and they're pillaging the land and terrorizing the local gentry along the way."

"Don't tell me—Tanner is heading south too."

"Already there. I guess the town's a chaotic mess,

and he and his men are trying to herd the stragglers who disobeyed the evacuation request into makeshift safety zones."

Solace glanced toward the town, black smoke streamed skyward in several places. She sent a silent *I love you, stay safe* to Tanner, as she tucked away her handheld. "A few civilian casualties and several soldiers wounded," she added. "And the hospital in town has been vacated, so the injured will be coming to Lance, which means he's going to be busy and not available for backup either."

"We're lucky to have him watching over us," Port said. "He'll take good care of the soldiers."

"I agree. He's one of the good ones. Look." Solace gave Port a nudge.

The enemy continued practicing tactical formations, but several other creatures now stood out as even more unusual than the rest. What had they gone and conscripted into their scaly ranks?

"They brought friends to the party." Port took her turn using the binoculars. "I can't tell yet what or who they are."

"Since we don't have backup, I guess we should maintain observation mode."

Noodge whined and inched forward. "Easy boy," Solace draped one arm over the huge animal, and leaned against him. "I don't like waiting either, big guy."

****

Malachi spun around and glanced toward the ridge rising up in front of the camp, his heart pounded in his chest. Port was there—he could feel her—and her other sister. They've come for Bliss. Not good, not good. A special ops mission wasn't the answer. If by a miracle the two of them made it in, the three of them would never make it out.

Muffled noises from inside the trailer, told him he better think of something fast. The time for declaring sides was now. He didn't care if he started a full-fledged war right this bloody minute, and he no longer cared what Mother had planned.

He dropped the illusion used to beautify the nearby house which Xandora occupied. Her wails of annoyance could be heard all the way over to the camp. Time to grow-up, your highness. No more simple tricks. He needed his energy. This was the big league. Then recalling his other promise to Mother, he relented and threw a spell of keeping over Xandora. It would remain until he or Mother decided otherwise.

Deploying wings, he shot up into the air, dropped his own protective cover, and started conjuring. Gorlock ran out of the trailer, a startled expression on his face. As he screamed chants into the air, the two-bit wizard twirled and danced and cursed. Malachi deflected every spell and charm with ease.

Thurax appeared next. His weaponry, non-ethereal, turned out to be just as useless against the shield wall Malachi had created. The big brute appeared as wily as ever though, and when he realized the futility of his approach, he changed tactics, rallying the nearby troops. Just whom did he intend to fight? Unless the Army E.T. squad showed up, there was really no one else for them to engage—accept Solace and Port. Had they been discovered?

Chapter Eleven

The marauding Reptiles had fought hard, but not hard enough. His unit had easily won the day.

"Good job men, secure the area," Tanner ordered.

He surveyed the town. Most of the residents had evacuated as advised. Long gone, they never came in contact with the enemy. The stubborn holdouts, however, were another story.

When the Reps showed up, they had predictably panicked, creating the traffic jam of the century. Now abandoned cars stood with doors ajar, their alarms wailing, their radios still playing. The effect was eerie.

A few town members paid for their foolishness with their lives, others had been found hiding and taken into protective custody. Some had seen too much. As soon as he could alert Mother to the situation, she would enhance the memory of those in need of mental comfort and wellbeing. When looking back they would recall a regular human enemy, not the Reps. He was glad for that. Like it or not, memories—good or bad—changed a person's life.

As he waited for his last group of men to check in, the need to wrap this up and go help Solace tore at him. He'd hoped she'd stay put until he and his men could head her way. They were partners, and should be fighting side by side. As he pictured her, a half-smile pulled at his mouth. Besides being kick-ass gorgeous, she was smart, and one heck of a warrior. She'd be okay. At least he prayed she would be.

A rogue Rep charged down Main Street. A blast from a RPG ended his forward progress. For a moment, flashbacks of the Middle East, and his first Army Ranger mission, careened through his mind. There had been civilians there too. What a nightmare. War really was hell, and now it had come to his own backyard. Never in his wildest dreams had he imagined he'd be leading a platoon down the streets of an American city. The mission remained the same, defend and destroy. An oxymoron, one of many created by the government.

His newly trained men had responded well as they faced off with their lizard enemy for the first time. Oh they were scared all right, he could smell it on them, but they fought back aggressively, obeying orders to the letter. He couldn't be more proud of them.

Confident this sector remained secure, he decided to personally check on the other two platoons which meant somehow circumventing the impassible streets.

As he set out on foot, a civilian on a motorcycle roared past, the rider's face white as a ghost. You could hear his screams over the growl of the engine. Making the mistake of looking back, the driver lost control of the Harley, hit a curb, and went flying.

Tanner ran forward to help, but the guy gained his feet, and still shrieking in terror, ran off. He'd obviously crossed paths with a Rep.

The motorcycle lay on its side, the engine still running. Commandeering the bike, Tanner mounted up, his Jericho 941 strapped to his hip, and a M4A1 carbine slung across his back. Hoping to find what had frightened the civilian, he revved the engine, and headed in the opposite direction from the running man.

****

When Thurax and Gorlock raced out of the semitrailer, Bliss' hopes had risen. Then this bozo had shown up.

She growled and hissed at the Rep sent to guard her. He only laughed, and she didn't blame him. All her powers were gone. She couldn't conjure wings, or cloak her image, or compel him to release her. And as far as her sisters, she'd given up hours ago hoping to reach them. The metal room must be shielded in some manner, and trying to break through made her head hurt.

At least the rain had stopped. She no longer heard it drumming on the roof. But that could be good news or bad. The inclement weather had kept things a little subdued, if you could call the camp turmoil subdued. Now the buffer was gone.

A lot of shouting and carrying on filtered in, and hearing the uproar and not knowing what was happening, made her all the more anxious. She'd really screwed up. How could she have been so careless as to be captured?

Keeping one foot planted on the ground, she kicked at the Rep with the other. Then for what felt like the hundredth time, she struggled against the rope holding her arms suspended over her head. Her hands were already growing numb, and although she knew her attempts were futile, it gave her a reason to move around. She needed to stay active, needed to keep the blood flowing.

Another guttural laugh echoed from her scaly watchdog. He avoided the kicks, and then dared to step closer. "Not so tough now are you, Fae Warrior."

He laid one clawed finger at the hollow of her neck, and watching her face, applied pressure. Sharp as a Fae dagger, the talon cut into her flesh. It went deep, and burned like fire, and beneath her clothing, a warm trickle of blood ran down her chest between her breasts. Damn his hide. If she could only get loose, she'd show him just what a Fae Warrior was capable of.

He continued to drag the claw downward, ripping the fabric of her blouse now stained blue with her blood. That infuriated her even more. The shade of dusty green went so well with her red hair, not all colors did. "Cut me loose and let's have at it," she challenged.

"Would if I could," he sneered. "In fact, if it were up to me, you'd be dead and the main course for lunch." He sniffed at her, and his lips curled back revealing sharp gleaming-white teeth. Mouth partially open, like a cat, he sucked in more air tasting and ingesting her scent.

She'd never spent much time up close and personal with a Rep, their usual interaction being quick and bloody and over as soon as possible. When analyzed from this perspective, the species took on an even more dreadful aspect. This one's eyes were nearly solid black, an endless void with no emotion. Only causing her pain seemed to animate his features.

Tired and hurting, she sagged farther away from the Rep. She'd taken a blow to the head before being brought in here, making it hard to concentrate. How odd. Crazy images swirled and danced before her, but her thoughts seemed to move in slow motion.

When his lizard tongue snaked out and touched the

tip of her nose, Bliss inhaled a deep, much needed, breath of air, and all her senses snapped back to high alert. He laughed as she jerked away, and she wished Noodge was here to take a big bite out of his green ass.

Her heart ached for her furry baby, and she hoped he was all right.

The uproar outside increased in intensity, catching both her attention and the Rep's. He leaped back as the door to the trailer burst open, and Thurax stepped through the opening.

Chapter Twelve

Being unable to communicate with Bliss worried Port to no end. Either a barrier of some type blocked their natural connection, or sorcery was involved. There was a third option, of course, but she wouldn't let her mind go there. Besides, if Bliss was dead, she'd know it.

At least Solace was by her side, she was glad for that. At the ranch, they had trained as a group, but just look at them now. They seemed so scattered, with each of their partners doing their own thing today.

Port opened the old tote bag Bliss had donated for carrying the laser shotguns especially fashioned for each of them. Keeping one for herself, she handed the other to Solace. Too bad Bliss didn't have hers. Instead it sat back at the ranch in the bedroom she shared with Nate. Hang on little sister, you'll soon be back with the man you love.

"What the heck. Are those Hover Rats?" Solace pointed to the sky, just to the left of the camp.

"Rattus Arrukus," Port agreed, "and flying rats isn't just an expression anymore. Those other creatures we saw must be Hover Rat wranglers. "

"They're carrying egg-bombs."

Port had run into these nasty creatures once before. The grenade-like weapons the winged vermin carried might sound cute, but they were deadly.

Glancing over her shoulder, Port's gaze skimmed across the valley to where Lance waited with his triage teams. They better stop these bomb-toting uber-mice, or there would be no place to take the wounded.

The skies began to clear, but as the swarm of Hover Rats took flight, they blocked out the long awaited sun. Big as dogs, they had vicious eagle-like claws, and a passel of huge teeth crammed into their pointy rat faces.

Maintaining a prone position, Solace fired, hitting the closest one still high overhead. The bomb he carried went off creating a midair explosion which knocked out two of his comrades. Slime and debris filled the air, raining down on them.

Port conjured utility wings, and took to the air, blasting away. A carcass slammed into the dirt where she'd been lying. The egg-bomb didn't go off. Solace pried it from the dead claws, and with a pitch Sandy Koufax would have been proud of, she tossed it at an incoming. The ensuing chain-reaction explosions knocked off another four flying rat-bastards. Changing tactics, one rat landed nearby, running toward Solace on a suicide mission.

Noodge bounded forward to head him off.

"No," Solace warned, the terror in her voice unmistakable. But this time the Rapran didn't listen. Not realizing the enemy had a bomb, their four-footed comrade headed straight for the Hover Rat. The explosion happen as the two made contact, the noise causing both sisters to shudder, their sensitive Fae ears quivering under the barrage of noise.

When the smoke cleared Noodge lay motionless on the ground, a nasty gash in his side—several less critical wounds also penetrating his thick hide. Port landed to protect him. Solace jumped up to do the same. Blasting away with their laser shotguns, their war cries filling the air, they stood tall seeking revenge on their winged enemy. They never flinched in the face of the onslaught, as they fended off assault after assault. Only after the area was littered with dead rats, and the ground was pocked marked from egg bomb explosions, did they cease fire.

At the call of their masters, the few remaining Rattus showed their pink hairless tails, and flew back the way they'd come.

Solace dropped to her knees beside Noodge, her silver tears falling on his fur. "Why wouldn't he listen, Port? Bliss will never forgive me."

"Take him to the field hospital. I'll wait here."

"I can't leave you alone."

"You can and you will. Don't argue," she added as Solace opened her mouth to speak, and no doubt disagree.

When Noodge whimpered like a kitten, the discussion came to a quick end.

"Give me your cargo jacket," Solace said, removing hers.

Arranging the Army issued gear side by side, they zipped the two jackets together and rolled Noodge onto the resulting square of fabric. Wrapping the camo material around him, they tied the sleeves into loops, then using their belts, they join it all together. The makeshift sling put compression on his wounds, and gave Solace something sturdy to grip.

"I'll be back as soon as possible." Solace created her strongest utility wings.

Port knew it would be a struggle to gain altitude with such a load. As her sister flew away, drops of Noodge's blood fell from the sky like red rain, leaving a trail behind her.

Tears welled in Port's eyes. Their darn courageous hairball meant more to her than she would ever admit. He had to be okay. Lance would save him. Swiping at her eyes with the back of one hand, she forced herself into warrior mode, standing guard on her perimeter. There would be time later to cry, or hopefully to rejoice and give thanks.

**** 

Thurax unsheathed the huge knife he wore at his side. Bliss braced for the fatal blow. Instead he swung the blade over her head, cutting the rope holding her wrists. Taken by surprise, she dropped to the ground, but didn't remain there long. He yanked her to her feet, dragged her across the floor, and threw her out the door. Hands still tied, she tumbled down the steps and landed in a heap. Ugh, why'd it have to be in stinky muddy slime?

Towering over her, wicked knife still at the ready, Thurax glared down at her. She tried conjuring wings— still without success. At least, no longer surrounded by the spell infused metal, she could sense her sisters were near. Studying the legions of Reps, she hoped Solace and Port were farther away than they felt. A commotion in the air had Thurax shaking his fist and roaring insults.

"Malachi, you twisted mother's son. Cease your battle with Gorlock, or the Fae dies." This time grabbing her by the hair, he hauled her to her feet. The routine was getting old fast.

Two figures battled, but not with conventional weapons. One had to be Malachi, and he was magnificent. Dressed in black, he hung in the air leisurely flapping huge wings of the same dark hue. She felt his controlled fury, if unleashed she suspected he could destroy half the mountain. Nearby, levitating only a few feet off the ground, Gorlock conjured spells, wildly flinging taunts and insults at Malachi.

She suspected this Gorlock character had frozen her powers. Now Malachi turned the tables doing the same to Gorlock as they engaged in a battle of wills.

As the tension rose to a palpable level, a banshee-like shrieking up on the mountain drew all their attention. It could only be Xandora.

Taking advantage of the distraction, Bliss wrenched free of Thurax, and began using him as a Mixed Martial Arts bag. Even with her wrists bound, her Dagda training served her well, and the startled expression on his brutal alien face transformed into a reflection of pain as her next kick connected with his crotch. He staggered in agony, and stumbled backward over a boulder. She moved closer to where Malachi hovered. He smiled in greeting and landed between her and Gorlock then he dissolved the ropes binding her hands and the spell binding her power.

"We need to get out of here"—he said—"now."

Still a bit shaky, Bliss conjured wings, grateful when Malachi took her by the hand and gave her an assist, as they launched skyward. Conventional bullets began to fly. All the shots went wild, not even coming close. Malachi must be bending the trajectory.

## Chapter Thirteen

Suddenly, as if a veil had been lifted, or a frayed cable had been repaired, Port connected to Bliss, full force. She felt Malachi too. But relief from knowing Bliss lived waned as concern for her staying in that condition took over. From her position, she couldn't see into the canyon, but she heard a lot of gunfire echoing up from the camp.

Mentally calling out to Bliss, Port let her know her position, then the growl of a vehicle approaching at her back intruded on her thoughts. She turned and watched as Lance came careening up the rocky slope in a Jeep. The 4x4 slid to a stop, and Dr. Lawson jumped out.

"How's Noodge," she asked, as he crouched down beside her.

"He's doing great. He needed eighty-four stitches. And I used some staples to reinforce the incision as I doubt once the anesthesia wears off he'll remain inactive. Luckily, he didn't lose as much blood as it first appeared. Because I have no idea what we could have used to transfuse him. A problem needing immediate research."

"And Solace, she's okay, landed safe?"

"Yes. She did an amazing job bringing him in. That big boy is solid muscle under all the hair. She opted to stay with Noodge until he's fully awake, which shouldn't be long as he was coming out of anesthesia surprisingly fast. The site where we had the IV is nearly mended already. These creatures have some amazing healing properties. Another area worth in-depth study."

"Okay, great. We can hypothesize later. Right now, we need to rescue Bliss."

"Solace filled me in. I figured sensible or not, you'd try some kind of heroics on your own," he accused, with a big smile. "That's why I'm here."

She noticed for the first time he'd traded scrubs for fatigues, and his scalpel for a rifle.

"Thank you."

"You're welcome. So what's the plan?"

She knew he'd seen plenty of action, had probably led many missions, yet he still bothered to ask what she had in mind. She appreciated his confidence in her. Now if she only had something brilliant in mind to offer in response.

"Getting close without being shot, pretty much sums it up."

"Then what?"

"Find Bliss and get her out."

"Rather devoid of details, but clear enough. How about we circle around to the far ridge. From there we should have a clear overall view of the camp. Solace described your skirmish with those Hover Rats. They wouldn't expect you to come from that direction."

"Sounds solid. Let's make like the birds, and get the flock out of here."

He laughed at her attempt to lighten the mood. For a Hume, he really was a great partner.

The terrain, rocky and uphill, presented only a minor challenge. Flying would have been easier, but she wanted to remain on the ground with Lance as long as possible. He'd definitely risen from *McMight Have Possibilities* to *McReally Great Guy*. She felt sorry for originally labeling him *McStudly*. He'd been nothing but kind to her, and on occasions fatherly. Again, unexpected, but appreciated.

Smoke from the numerous campfires obscured the air, but as they reached the intended ridge, she could make out Malachi and Bliss rising out of the valley. Thank Jupiter, they were safe. Thurax stood roaring in frustration, and a scrawny magician ran back and forth below like a frightened child.

Port relaxed, and she and Lance held their position as the other two drew near, leaving imminent danger behind. But her next breath caught in her throat as Malachi swooped in on black wings.

Tattered and smoldering, he landed before her. Bliss eased to the ground at his side.

She reached for Bliss, hugging her tight, but her gaze lingered on Malachi's face. His beautiful *dangel* face—part danger, part angel. He set her blood on fire, and the love they once shared rushed at her as if it were only yesterday they had been together, as if no separation had occurred.

Using a supreme effort, she shifted her attention once more to Bliss, but a part of her stayed behind with him, the connection, now reestablished wouldn't easily be broken.

She studied the bruising on her sister's face and wrists, and winced. How many more injuries lurked beneath her clothing? Poor thing, she would be the one needing the Saturnalia cream tonight. Then she remembered how worried everyone had been, and anger trumped sympathy.

"What in blue heaven were you thinking? We—"

"I know. I'm sorry," Bliss interrupted. "Besides, who are you to talk? You snuck away earlier without any harm, and I only did it to get the two of you together." Bliss nodded toward Malachi. "And look, it worked."

"Well it was a darn high price to pay," Port snapped back. "Almost a fatal one."

As if to avoid additional reprimands, Bliss scurried sideways to stand behind Lance, leaving Port alone and face to face with Malachi.

"So," she huffed, looking him up and down, "how about you, are you all right? Not that I care." Dang why'd she have to add the last bit. He'd know it was a lie, and it sounded so petty and whiny.

"Never better."

"Liar. You look terrible."

Not true either. The smudges of darkness beneath those golden eyes said he was worn out and needed to re-energize, but they didn't detract from his handsome features.

"Where's everybody else?" he asked, ignoring her taunt. "What's the plan for taking out these misfits?"

One thing for sure, you could never accuse Malachi of beating around the bush. But at his question, silence reigned.

"I see," he said, with a nod of understanding. "None of you trust me. Can't blame you I suppose, since I just came from the enemy camp."

*I want to trust you.* The female part of her screamed out the words. *I love you, and I need you back in my life.* Then the warrior in her reminded Port it wasn't her decision alone to make.

"Not my call." She glanced at Bliss and Lance.

"He protected me down there, Port. I was heading for the last rodeo."

"Last round up," Lance corrected, patting her arm in a paternal gesture as he stepped forward.

The Sisters of Anu seemed to have become the *daughters* of Dr. Lawson. It was nice, it felt good. But as he stood face to face with Malachi, the fatherly aura dropped away and some sort of testosterone-infused atmosphere erupted followed by a mono e mono display. Like a standing stone, Malachi towered over Dr. Lawson, but her Hume partner never blinked. Way to go Lance, because Malachi could be downright scary.

"He does seem a rather questionable character," Lance noted, over his shoulder, "and I'm not keen on the magic angle. But on the other hand, he just saved Bliss. I say he's in."

"Why thank you, Dr. Lawson. And may I say, although I find some of your medical practices rather barbaric, I know your intentions are good."

"Well played." Lance chuckled, slapping Malachi on the back.

What the heck just happened? Were they best buds now? It had to be a male thing. Of course, with or without spells and enchantments, Malachi had a way of charming nearly all beings. He appeared larger than life, in more ways than one. An intergalactic pirate with tales to tell. An adventurer of many worlds with promises in his eyes.

Those golden eyes had been the beginning of the end for her. At least that's what she had always professed. Now she hoped they were the beginning of something new, with no end in sight.

"Are you sure neither of you requires medical attention," Port pressed, trying to get everybody back on track. "My partner's a damn good doctor. He did a great job sewing up Noodge."

Dang, she'd meant to ease into that information, not blurt it out.

"Noodge... What happened, where is he?" Bliss took on a whiter shade of pale, making her bruises stand out even more noticeably.

"Oh, honey, he's okay. He knew you were in trouble, and led us here. Then we came under attack by a horde of Hover Rats. He saved us from a direct egg-bomb hit, and got hurt in the process. Solace took him to Lance's triage center."

"He's doing fine, Bliss," Lance reassured. "I wouldn't have left his side if I thought otherwise. Solace and Nurse Montgomery are watching over him."

"I thought he was near." Bliss turned in the direction of the field hospital, one hand reaching out as if to touch Noodge's spirit. "And I thought he might be hurt. I should have realized, should have asked about him first thing."

"I'm guessing being strung up and soundly beaten has your mind a tad off kilter," Malachi offered.

"He's more than just my four-footed partner. It's my job to worry about him."

"He's going to be fine, I promise," Lance reaffirmed. "In fact, before I left, I noticed some of his minor wounds were already starting to heal. Like I told Port, his powers of regeneration are remarkable."

"My little baby is exceptional in so many ways."

"Your little baby nearly broke the surgical table,"

Lance said, with a shake of his head and a hardy laugh. "A good lesson indicating we need sturdier equipment. Why even the likes of Malachi would strain some of our portable equipment. Working with otherworldly entities, we should have taken such into consideration."

"I suppose you'd like to work on a Rep too," Port teased.

"A nice autopsy would be appreciated. The two aliens you took-out in the woods were destroyed by the E.T. Squad. I didn't get a look at them. And I have to admit, except for the war part, this has been a fascinating experience."

\*\*\*\*

Within hours, Noodge recovered enough to be moved, and with the enemy camp in turmoil, it seemed an opportune time to head back to the Ranch.

Nate remained in his lab continuing to work on his newest project. When he'd heard Bliss had gone missing, he'd interrupted his plans until being assured she was safe. Now there were a few things he needed to finish up. That meant only Captain Jackson was off the premises as they gathered in the dining room.

"Did everybody survive the pillaging in Colorado Springs?" Port asked, as Solace ended her most recent call to Tanner.

"Unfortunately, no. The town is a wreck. Five civilian casualties, and five soldiers injured."

Gaining his feet, Lance grabbed his hat and medical backpack.

"It's okay, Doc," Solace said. "This time they're taking the wounded to Fountain City."

"I'm still responsible to oversee their care," he contested.

"It's pretty far away," Port pointed out, "and we may need you here."

Relenting Lance sat back down as Alfonso entered the room.

"Tanner said they would head back this way as soon as they could," Solace informed the little man who kept their bellies full, and their spirits up. "That means a lot of mouths to feed."

"No problem," Alfonso reassured, setting out a tray of fresh fruits and veggies, and two different kinds of dips. "In the old days, when we ran cattle, we often fed many men during branding and roundup season. Nobody eats more than a hungry vaquero. Natty will be here soon, too?" he asked. A veil of worry overshadowed his expression.

"He's on the property," Bliss reassured, "putting up his equipment. The device he's invented will be a big help."

Alfonso smiled and stood a little taller, his concern fading. "I'd better get back to the kitchen then," he said, taking his leave.

Those gathered in the dining room, discussed details from today's events. Port glanced at Malachi. He'd played a huge part in helping their team today. Now he hung back in the shadows, as if he felt like an outsider.

When they settled into a comfortable silence, Port gained her feet.

"I need some air," she announced, on the way out of the room.

Knowing Malachi would follow, she waited on the porch, aware of his presence the minute he appeared.

"What do you suppose Xandora will try next?" she

asked.

"The only thing I'm sure of is she won't give up easily. She's obsessed with either taking over Earth or destroying it. And I wonder if she really cares which comes to pass."

"Were you with her only because Mother assigned you to watch her?" She stood tall, bracing for the answer. What if he'd been at her side for months, maybe all of the three years they'd been apart? What if he had feelings for her?

"By the gods, woman. That you even have to ask, wounds me."

"She's very beautiful, based on the paintings I've seen, and we've been apart a long time." It felt like forever.

"Yes, well doing one's duty, regardless of the task, has nothing to do with you or me. Light-years may have separated us physically, but nothing ever came between or lessened my love for you, Portence.

He stepped closer and turned her around. She felt as if she'd jumped headfirst into his amber eyes—eyes glowing with intensity and desire. Her wing ports twitched, and her tattoos glowed. Dang she should have worn a turtleneck sweater, or a jacket, anything but this low cut blouse revealing how turned on she was. He bent and kissed the protection sign he'd given her as she lay helpless in the hospital. The gentle touch resonated all the way to the tip of her toes.

He straightened, and placed his hands on her shoulders. "I'm sorry you lost our baby."

Pain, surprise, and anger clashed inside of her, and a muted sound encompassing all three escaped her lips. She hadn't told anyone, not even her sisters. Maybe

Mother—She tried to pull away, but he held fast, keeping her in place.

"How did you know?" she asked, finding her voice.

"That's the very reason I ignored your heroic demands of staying with me and the ship. I thought by sending the two of you to the trash planet, I was sending both of you to safety. When the trawler took a hit, delaying its ability to reach you, a piece of my heart died. The piece that had been so thankful we were going to share such a glorious experience—one rather rare as I'm not full-blooded Fae."

At her stunned silence, he continued.

"The agony of knowing you were in trouble and I could not reach you nearly destroyed me as I drifted in space. I could think of nothing else. It haunts me to this day."

Tears filled her eyes and ran down her cheeks. The loss of the child haunted her as well. All this time she hated Malachi for abandoning her, for being instrumental in the loss of the baby she hadn't known at the time she carried. And all along he'd been trying to save them both.

He reached up and wiped away her tears. The silver glowed on his fingertips, and waving his hand in the air, he turned the tears to fireflies.

"When did you know?" she asked, taking his hand in hers.

"The very night it happened."

"But…"

"I thought it only right for you to discover the miracle on your own, and to decide when you wanted to tell the world, and more importantly when you wanted

Gini Rifkin

to tell me. After we were separated, Mother said to stay away, that you were too upset to see or speak to me, so I did her bidding across time and space, always hoping you would eventually come to me."

Port shook her head. "Mother told me when you'd finally been found, you needed time to recover from drifting so long in the Absolute Zone. Then she assigned us missions in totally opposite ends of the Multiverse."

"Would you have been ready before now to listen, or to forgive?"

"No," she admitted. "I suppose not. But carrying such anger and hatred for so long did little to edify my soul."

"And *my* unrelenting guilt and regret did little to expand mine—a true shame as my soul sorely needed work to begin with."

She smiled as she slid into his waiting embrace, allowing his warmth to wrap her in hope and expectation.

After a moment, he took a step back, and the desire in his eyes slammed through her like a physical touch. "I'll not wait any longer for you," he declared.

Hands raised, palms touching, their fingers interlaced. Her heart pounded in her chest, anticipating what was to come, anticipating what she had thought never to experience again. Gazes locked on one another, they conjured wings simultaneously, and slowly rose off the ground.

A wicked smile curved his tempting mouth, and her clothes disappeared. She laughed and eased closer to him. His clothes disappeared, too, and warm skin against warm skin, higher and higher they gained altitude, disappearing into the night sky.

"I didn't think it possible," he murmured, "but here in my arms, your beauty surpasses even my most cherished memories of you. You are my breath, my heartbeat, my reason to live."

As darkness engulfed them, her tattoos glowed brightly, and at his words, if felt as if her heart took flight. She'd never stopped loving him. Even when she wished him a fate worse than death, part of her needed him, desired him.

She wrapped her arms around his neck, and his mouth found hers, taking, giving, exploring, owning. Her skin came alive beneath his touch as his hands slid from her shoulders downward to her thighs. He urged her to wrap her legs around his body, and accommodating the notion, arms now braced against his chest, she leaned back offering herself to him. He stroked her breasts, teasing one nipple then the other, bringing both to taut peaks.

Wings flapping leisurely, they slowly spun around and around, and his touch glided across her form as if she were a cherished instrument he intended to play to exhaustion. He knew what turned her on. Knew what gave her the greatest pleasure, the deepest delight, what brought her to the brink.

They gained more altitude, and then hung in the air horizontally, both sets of wings moving just enough to keep them aloft. He leaned over her, one hand nestled at the small of her back, the other continuing to pleasure her with demanding touches. Loosening the grip of her legs, she reached down to please him in kind, and a groan of enjoyment escaped him. His warm breath teased across her throat before he bit at her neck sending shivers convulsing through her from head to toe.

Both hands now gripping her waist, he growled as if overcome by the need to have all of her, and he made them one in body and heart. Head thrown back she cried out, and feet locked at his back, she pressed closer, driving him deeper. Remaining intimately connected, they went vertical, their wings working harder, matching their rising desire.

Finding their rhythm, he delved deeply, only to retreat and take her again and again. As they flew higher, the atmosphere grew cold, but the heat of their passion kept them warm. Mouths locked on one another, he took her senses along with her body to even greater height.

Soaring into the heavens, her breath came in fits and starts, and she knew what they sought couldn't be far off. When his breathing matched hers, she wrapped her arms around his neck, furled her wings, and held on tight. He enfolded his black feathered wings around the both of them, and in that spectacular final moment, as they found the greatest pleasure, they plummeted toward earth locked in a lover's embrace.

The air rushed around them as they dropped faster and faster, and putting all her faith and trust in him, Port reveled in the waves of delight racking her body. Turning around and around, plunging downward so fast she could barely catch a breath, the ground far below, seemed to rush up to meet them, and the free-fall sensation doubled the excitement, driving her beyond mere gratification. Just before they crashed to earth, he set his wings, bringing them to a soft landing in a small stand of quaking aspen. Still clinging to one another, they collapsed to the ground.

Flushed and satisfied and laughing like children, they scrambled to their feet and sought the shelter of a rustic arbor. The last autumnal hurrah of morning glories decorated the archway which accommodated a swing strewn with colorful pillows. Malachi materialized caftans for each of them. Black for him, a smoky blue for her. Surprisingly, she enjoyed the bit of color, and knowing he would never relinquish his claim to the mysterious persona he had created, she figured she'd better choose a new favorite color other than black.

Easing down onto the swing, she urged him to join her, and with one arm around her shoulder, he snugged her near.

"Promise me we will never be separated again," he demanded.

"I promise," she said, and meant it with every beat of her heart, and every fiber of her soul.

For a moment, they sat quietly side by side, perfectly content, just like any normal couple in love.

Of course they were far from normal, which she truly preferred.

## Chapter Fourteen

"You owe me." Xandora's voice, sharp and cold, clashed with the hot spark of anger flashing in her eyes.

Hephaestus sighed. He should have been more careful with the scraps left over from making Pandora. But that was an error from long ago. Giving in to Xandora's rantings and coming here, constituted a recent mistake, possibly of equal proportion.

He blamed his foolish decision on being bored, for he had been, almost to tears. And in Xandora's psychopathic mind, and by sibling proxy, she obviously deemed it her right to demand his help. He supposed in a way he did owe her, and could at least listen to what she had to say. Besides, now that he was here, he might as well make the best of it.

"I need you to create a palace for me," she demanded, in a slightly more harmonious tone. "You had one on Olympus, I want one too. And we need weapons. I've more soldiers now, enough to take the mountain, but their hands are empty."

So, she hadn't given up on commandeering the underground facility, a plan doomed to failure. Like much of the galaxy in the know, he'd heard about events from afar. Even Spacebook carried bits and pieces—the information sketchy and oftentimes written-off as hoax. "You have troops across the planet," he encouraged, hoping she would rethink her strategy. "Why not concentrate on them?"

"Not any more, except for a few strongholds, they're gathering here. Spread so thin they were losing ground. This is our red line. We win or die here."

Demanding, delusional, and deceitful—yet fearless in battle. And now obsessed to a lethal degree with becoming a legend, no matter who got killed in the process.

"The mountain command center is our primary objective," she insisted. "From inside the rock fortress, I can rule the world!" Arms thrust out as if to embrace the global realm she sought to govern, Xandora's eyes sparkled overly bright, and her cheeks grew ruddy.

Having abandoned her wooden hovel, she now resided in a large tent with carpets on the floor, and colored cloth on the walls. And as she declared war, with her bold as brass attitude, she could have been mistaken for a young Helen of Troy.

Ahh Helen. He hadn't thought about his sister for quite some time.

Xandora lowered her arms, and snapped her fingers in front of his face to gain his attention. "My troops," she said, grasping a new thought by the throat, "are quite ferocious, but they'll rule no one without armaments. You can create all the weapons we need. You fashioned a winged helm and sandals for Hermes, a chariot for Helios, a magic girdle for your unfaithful wife Aphrodite. The list goes on and on. And I want something special just for me. I want a flying horse, so I can take to the sky like those ugly Fae witches."

"Sorry, there is only one Pegasus, and he's not for you."

Having had her wish so flatly denied, she fumed

and stomped, her limp becoming obvious. He thought of his own leg, less than perfect, and pity pulled at him. All her life she'd been second best. He supposed he could make something appropriate for her.

He truly had created many wonders in his day. With a chuckle he recalled the throne of gold he'd created for Hera, his mother. His retribution had been complete when she became trapped in the regal chair. He hated his mother almost as much as he hated Zeus, but he failed to see how an alliance with Xandora aided his never-ending mission of making his wretched parents miserable. On the other hand, sticking it to Mother Nature sounded like good fun. She'd had no right to create Xandora in the first place, and behind his back to boot.

"Then make me a flying bed." The curious new demand interrupted his thoughts. Xandora clapped her hands and twirled around. "One with a canopy to keep off the sun. I can command my subjects without even getting up in the morning."

By the gods, if nothing else one had to admire Xandora's audacity.

Botu, leader of her Reptiles, and Thurax approached—a welcome interruption. What hideous beasts they were, and Hephaestus recognized hideous when he saw it. He'd cultivated a long and successful relationship with Polyphemus, the Cyclops—a good friend, but no cover model.

Verbally sparring, these two appeared on the verge of coming to blows. When he'd first arrived on earth, after giving in to Xandora's unceasing and intolerable pleading, he'd come across the vicious creatures at one another's throats. It would be helpful if they would temporarily put aside their differences. He waited for one of them to speak.

"What do you plan to do now?" Thurax fired the question at Xandora as if it were a mortar shell. "We must strike soon. Your troops grow restless."

"How dare you use such a tone with me, you green-haired imbecile. And where is the useless magician you boasted would be of such help to our cause? For a famed mercenary, you have yet to impress me with your brains or your brawn. You let the Fae escape, and she took Malachi with her."

"You stupid female, *Malachi* took *her*."

As soon as the words were out of his mouth, it appeared Thurax knew it had been a mistake. Xandora had been operating under the impression Malachi had been kidnapped or somehow taken against his will. To admit he left of his own accord would fracture her psyche even more.

She slid a dagger from her belt, and with the weapon raised, launched herself in the direction of the big warrior.

Catching her around the waist, Hephaestus held her back. "Let's concentrate on killing the enemy, shall we?"

To his surprise, she stilled and appeared to actually consider his advice. Wrenching free, and no doubt wishing it was Thurax's chest, she stabbed the knife into the scarred top of a nearby table. Then with a murderous expression she started issuing commands.

"You, Botu, don't just stand there, go muster the troops."

"He couldn't muster a pack of dogs," Thurax, growled, daring to speak again. "Several of his soldiers are AWOL. The others toy with the idea of rebelling against him—and you. They're plotting his downfall as we speak. Put me in charge of the soldiers."

The Reptile commander snarled and shook his lizard head as if in disbelief. "They left because you whip them for minor offenses. They need discipline not blind cruelty."

The two top guns stepped toward one another, the specter of death in both sets of eyes.

"Enough," Hephaestus bellowed. "This infighting is getting us nowhere. You're more ill-mannered than my calamitously children, even worse than Cupid. This rabble army needs to get its Reptile shit together, and that includes the two of you. You can kill each other later."

Taking a step apart, the silent behemoths exchanged glares while Hephaestus assessed the odds of them winning this invasion. He had his sources too, and they reported that while a few civilians had been terminated, and a few human soldiers had been wounded, those left in the Army E.T. squad remained formidable, disciplined, and regrouping. The Reptile army outnumbered the humans, but with the Fae as allies, it helped even the score. The death toll on both sides could be heavy.

Of course, being immortal, he had nothing to fear, and little to lose, only time—and his patience. His gaze fell on Xandora.

"I'll need my minions and forge. And my new apprentice robot, Talos 2.0"

\*\*\*\*

That evening, Tanner's men set up camp and a perimeter guard on the vast ranch property. Their bellies were full thanks to Alfonso, and those with injuries not requiring a trip to the hospital in Fountain City, had been treated by Dr. Lawson.

The weary seven, including Malachi, finished eating, and while Alfonso cleared the table at the main house, they headed for the war room cabin. Time for the usual end of the day debriefing.

Walking at Malachi's side, Port inhaled his scent. Tired and well fed, daydreaming could hardly be avoided, and memories of drifting off to sleep while being held in his arms sneaked into her thoughts. This would never do. Loosening the jacket she wore, she invited the cold to surround her. The coolness refreshed and revived her senses, and with a deep breath of night air, she tried replacing the past with the here and now.

Although stiff and limping slightly, Noodge refused to be left behind, and after they entered the cabin and shut the door, the Rapran took command of his usual spot guarding the portal. Tonight, he sat at full attention, his face totally Rapacious Ranivorous fierce, as if to challenge anyone who might think him not fit for duty.

Then as if by magic, Nate's cat, Mrs. Maxwell, appeared. In the barn, on property, or around the house, she ruled. And even for a feline, her ability to silently come and go seemed exceptional. Strutting over to Noodge, she wove her body back and forth between his front legs. He lowered his head as if to push her away, but rather than take the hint, she gave his face a good licking. An expression of mortification wilted his ferocious demeanor. When she curled up at his feet, he gave a sigh, scooped her closer, and lay down, making sure not to squash her.

After today's events, it seemed they were all in need of comfort. A luxury Port intended to take advantage of in the future since she had let down her emotional shields.

"Here you go, Malachi," Tanner said, adding another chair to the ones already at the table.

After Captain Jackson found out Malachi was Special Ops, like he'd been in his Ranger days, Tanner had quickly come around to accepting the Fae/sorcerer. But what about the others? However, her doubts faded when everybody scooched around making sure Malachi had enough room. What a nice way for the rest of them to welcome him into the group. Their little tribe of eclectic beings.

****

Finished analyzing today's events from each perspective, they were about to leave when the Mother board blipped. The room fell silent, all attention refocused in that direction. A brightly colored tropical scene filled the entire screen, wonderfully out of place considering they were eight thousand feet above sea level.

"Hello, troops," Mother began. "I see Malachi has joined your ranks—as it should be," she acknowledged. "It's my understanding, the battle is set for tomorrow."

The finality of her words came as a bit of a shock. Port glanced at the faces surrounding her. They all knew things were about to pop, but to hear it put into words, made it all too real.

"As you are now aware, Xandora includes in her ranks the mercenary Thurax, and Gorlock the magician—and I use the latter term lightly," she added, as if able to see Malachi bristle. "And today she's added a new face, actually an exceedingly old face, but new to some of you. Hephaestus has decided to join her."

"*The* Hephaestus?" Solace asked.

"Yes."

"Who's he?" Tanner asked. "By the look on your face, babe, I'm guessing I'm not going to like the answer."

Solace gave a *you explain it* nod to Bliss. A smart move as Bliss loved Greek mythology.

"From what I remember," Bliss began, her face serious with concentration, "Hephaestus began his life on Olympus, the son of Zeus and Hera. The family, being totally dysfunctional, weathered legendary and frequent fights. It remains unclear which parent threw Hephaestus off of the mountain, but he landed on a Greek island where he learned blacksmithing. Some say he was born with a crippled leg, and to this day walks with a limp. Other say the injury occurred when he fell to Earth.

"During a lull in the family squabbling, his mother set him up with Aphrodite. This may have been done for spite rather than out of kindness. After Hephaestus married Aphrodite, his new wife promptly cheated on him with his brother Ares."

"Makes for a fascinating Ancient Greek soap opera," Nate said, "but how does this impact us right now?"

"Hephaestus can forge many wonderful things," Bliss explained, "and many dreadful things—even Zeus's thunderbolts."

"Mother," Solace said, "is having a lesser god aiding the enemy fair? Sounds like a ringer, and a huge disadvantage for our team."

"I'll try to keep him busy. He has a bone to pick with me" Mother replied. "And I with him. And don't forget, Malachi can alter the course of bullets, bending their trajectory. That should help even the playing field. Hephaestus will have to come up with something non-traditional."

"With or without old Heph," Bliss encouraged, "We can beat those Rep-turds.

"It's supposed to be Rep-toads." Port corrected, with a laugh. Malachi cocked one brow, along with the questioning look he gave her. "It's an insult, as toads are amphibians. But Rep-turds works too."

"Regardless of what you call them," Mother interjected, "since we can't have the U.S. Army lobbing mortar shells and missiles at will, we're looking at hand to hand. So here is what we are going to do.

"Weapons on Xandora's side will be crude but effective. However, I believe Tanner's ground forces, with the aid of you ladies, will be sufficient to mount a successful mission. The ranks of the Hover Rats have been reduced considerably, but they still have a few egg bombs. Malachi will be in charge of curtailing any pseudo-magic thrown at us by Gorlock. Dr. Lawson, I need you ready to fight, but also available for the injured. Nate, your aerial reconnaissance will be appreciated, and your new invention will be invaluable. In your absence, Noodge will partner up with Bliss."

"How are things going in other parts of the country, or for that matter around the world?" Tanner asked.

"In general, much more quiet, mostly because so many of the enemy have relocated here. However, I hesitate to free up the Fae Warriors assigned across the globe. It could be a ploy to draw them off, or Xandora could change strategies on a whim. Should they become officially available, I'll send them this way, but don't count on it when planning your offense or defense. Be ready for combat in the morning. Any other questions?"

The room remained silent.

"One more thing, then." Mother's voice cut through their thoughts. "No one goes airborne until the battle begins."

Port's gaze darted over to Malachi, and she pursed her lips to disguise an unstoppable smile.

His unabashed grin had her squirming in her chair.

Chapter Fifteen

Using the new information, they reassessed their strategy and the logistics of deploying forces in the field. Forty minutes later, they filed out of the cabin and made for the main house.

Everyone drifted off in pairs, except for Dr. Lawson. A pang of guilt for ignoring her Hume partner nagged at Port. He shouldn't be alone tonight.

"Lance," she called, as he ambled by. "Want to hang out for a while?"

He smiled and shook his head. "I've been invited to smoke cheroots and drink tequila on the back porch with Alfonso. It's a good night for sharing war stories and memories," he added, appearing content with his plans. As Malachi walked up, Lance gave her a wink. "It's a good night for making new memories too." Without a backward glance, he sauntered off.

Alone with her magic man, Port led him to a stand of cottonwoods. Dark and secluded, she turned to face him, her back against the sturdy tree trunk, the heady fall fragrances exciting her senses. Malachi drew closer, his amber eyes reflecting the little light available.

"Sorry we can't take to the sky," she said, tracing a finger down the front of his body from neck to waist. Conquering her addiction for Malachi had been hard won, and so easily regained. After again partaking of him fully, she was hooked. Her need for him constant, and strong as ever. In fact, she couldn't keep her hands off of him.

"I think we can make do with terra firma," he said, the expression in his eyes assuring her the hypothesis would soon be tested.

She slipped out of her jacket allowing it to slide from her shoulders. He unbuttoned the top she wore beneath it. Hot desire clashed with cold air, each doing its best to take her breath away. She'd changed back into more practical clothing, and always seeking freedom, she'd gone commando—both top and bottom, and his tiger eyes burned brighter at the sight of her naked breasts. Strong hands caressed and aroused. Her wingports twitched, sending her mind, if not her body, sky-high.

Exploring inside the long coat he now wore, she grazed her fingertips across the fabric covering his chest. The heavy shirt didn't mask the rock solid flesh waiting beneath. They stared at one another, and the love in his eyes helped heal the remaining emotional scars. Little by little her heart had mended, and it felt lifesaving. Reaching up, she cradled his ruggedly handsome face. A face once responsible for her happiest moments. A face also responsible for the saddest time in her life.

As if to soothe the flash of painful memories he knew she harbored, Malachi gently ran his fingers through her hair. Then he abruptly changed tactics, and fisting her locks in his hands, he crushed his mouth down on hers. Meeting his cosmic craving, she parted her lips, seeking to please, but also to take.

Releasing her, he shrugged out of his long coat, and spread it at her feet. She took the hand he offered when he knelt and urged her to follow. As they lay side by side, raw hunger building fast, she unzipped his black trousers, releasing the part of him she wanted to, needed to, feel deep inside of her. To that end, she loosened and shimmied out of her own pants.

Skillfully teasing and tormenting, he spoke of things to come, then drawing her atop his body, he gave her what she wanted most, to be one with him.

Straddling his thighs, her head tilted back, she could see the stars through the multicolored leaves. Her wingports twitched, and although they were earthbound, Malachi made it seem as if they were flying. To enhance the illusion, she conjured sleek white wings of lattice work. Light and fragile as spun glass, they were useless, but gorgeous, and they made her feel pretty.

Hands braced on his shoulders she studied his face, and gazes locked, minds devoid of thoughts other than pleasing one another, they mentally reached for the stars, higher and higher. He led the way, demanding she follow to the end, and when he whispered, "Always mine," he took them both there. She lost track of everything—except the extraordinary way she felt.

Malachi's declaration sent her emotions as well as her body riding high—everything was going to be ducks and drakes. She eighty-sixed her wings, and smiled at the nearly forgotten phrase as she collapsed and lay upon his chest, his arms snugging her close, his breathing still quick and deep. But words said in the heat of battle, or the heat of passion, needed actions to prove their merit. Yet, it was certainly a good start to their new future together.

Struggling to their feet, they clung to one another,

and as the cool night coaxed a shiver from her body, she leaned closer to Malachi. He conjured black wings lined in cotton wool, and wrapped her in warmth and love.

**** 

The wake-up capsule Port swallowed the night before now became active, sending a not unpleasant tingling through her body. Still sleepy, she recalled other tingly pleasures recently enjoyed. But there wasn't time for reminiscing. She needed to get a move on.

Sitting up, she stretched, and then sliding from bed, padded over to the window to check on the weather. The pre-dawn light limited the view, but it appeared foggy. It would probably burn off once the sun came up.

Her two sisters still slept peacefully. By group consensus, and in hopes of everyone getting a good night's sleep, they had split up by gender, accept for Noodge. He belonged with the Fae Warrior team. Besides, separating him from Bliss *again* seemed unlikely.

With a sigh, she recalled when they were young, sometimes sleeping together in the tree bed, they'd had long talks in the dark of night, and wonderful pillow fights in the morning light.

Bliss' laugh came too late to warn her as a pillow hit her in the head.

"I was thinking of old times too," she said, her empath skills obviously switched on.

Minds again thinking alike, they both fired billowy missiles at Solace. Not fully awake, she took two direct hits. Port supposed it was silly for full-grown Warrior

Women to act so childishly, but by Jupiter it was fun. All three now on their feet, they each grabbed the nearest feather-filled weapon and went at it. Noodge harked and ran around, his special howling-bark meaning he felt happy too.

When the clanging of the kitchen triangle broke through their laughter, they called a truce, and out of breath, retreated to their respective bunks.

Solace checked her watch and grabbed her battle gear, "Alfonso must have been up all night if he already has breakfast on."

"He sure takes good care of us," Bliss agreed, lacing up her combat boots.

"I'll say, and there's nothing worse than going into battle on an empty stomach." Port buttoned her jumpsuit made of night Mandra camo cloth. It counted as wearing regulation equipment, yet mollified her near obsession with black clothing. Now she realized wearing this color had become her fetish only after being separated from her black haired partner. It seemed all along she had been trying to keep him near. By the gods she loved her dark sorcerer.

They clamored down the steps and headed for the dining area. Thinking about what the day might hold, her stomach did a flip-flop. Why? She'd gone into battle with Malachi many times, fought at his side. They'd always come out winners. But they had just gotten back together, and knowing the pain of losing him for a few years, she couldn't bear the thought of losing him for a lifetime.

With a shake of her head, she beat the thought to a pulp. They were all warriors, and none of them would change what they did. At least she wouldn't and neither would he. Wasn't it part of why they loved each other, part of the adventure? Yet, sometimes, a vision of a different life occurred to her. One where they were living open and free and not running toward danger—or from it. But these were crazy thoughts, and so unlike her. Maybe being poisoned and almost dying had rearranged her way of thinking, kindling these odd ideas.

Plates at the ready, the three of them shuffled along the sideboard, selecting items from the sumptuous buffet. Not knowing when another chance for food would come today, Port filled her plate and stuck a muffin in her pocket.

"Some of the food's already gone," she noted, glancing around for signs of the men. They must have already eaten. She spotted Noodge sitting contentedly by the door. He'd obviously eaten too.

"They were up even before me," Alfonso said, anticipating her question as he brought in a pot of tea. "After chowing down, they couldn't sit still. They're reconnoitering their assigned positions, and said to tell you they would meet you on the battlefield."

Eager as the men to get this over and done, the females shoveled food into their mouth as they walked toward the table and took to their chairs.

"Slow down, ladies," Alfonso advised, with a chuckle.

Literally dressed to kill, being called ladies brought smiles all around. But heeding Alfonso's advice, Port took a deep breath to curb the adrenaline flow. Food might be necessary fuel, but not good if it triggered indigestion.

"If all goes well, tomorrow at this time, it will all

be over," Solace mused.

Bliss reached for the syrup and poured it on her French toast. "A reassuring thought, yet sad. Who knows where we'll each be assigned next."

"I don't want to think about it," Solace said, and giving Bliss a pretend shove, she stole some of her honeydew melon.

As they finished eating, Port didn't want to think about it either.

Flying side by side, spirits high, they set off to the perimeter of the battlefield. Noodge ran along beneath them, easily keeping pace. His wounds completely healed.

They all wore laser pistols, and each one carried an additional preferred weapon. Solace chose a second pistol, Bliss a crossbow, and Port went totally old school with her atlatl. Thanks to Nate, they also each had a laser shotgun slung across one shoulder. They were ready to face down anything.

When Port pulled up short, Bliss and Solace followed suit. They hung in the air waiting for her to speak.

"We were separated by command not choice," she said, still wrestling with her previous worries. "In the future, if we choose to go our separate ways, please promise we will stay in touch. You are both part of me, just as I am part of you. I love you both so much." There, she'd said it out loud, such few words meaning so much.

"We love you too," Solace said.

"Now that Mother has allowed us contact with one another," Port persisted, "just promise me we won't lose track of one another."

"Look who's being sentimental," Solace teased.

Bliss scowled at Solace. "We promise," she said, in a serious tone. She seemed more to understand the deeper meaning attached to the words, and what it took for Port to express them.

When she'd been brokenhearted and mad at the Multiverse, the forced separation between herself and her sisters had been made to order. All she wanted was to be left alone. But ever since Bliss had tamed the troubles haunting her mind, the walls of protection were no longer needed. She had always loved her sisters, and shouldn't have been afraid to admit needing them, or anyone.

"Okay." Solace reaffirmed, no more laughing or teasing. "We promise."

"We're the sisters of Anu," Bliss reminded. "A bond stronger than distance or time."

Still aloft, they clasped hands, and chanted, "To the power of three, so shall it be."

"All for one and one for all," Solace added.

"Like female musketeers." Excited by the reference, Bliss let go and clapped her hands and laughed. "What a great idea."

"Oh no, now see what you've done," Port pretended to reprimand. "Next she'll suggest we wear plumed hats and carry rapiers."

"The hat sounds nice," Bliss countered, adjusting the bedazzled mini-tote attached to her belt. "It doesn't hurt to look your best going into battle. Although a sword is definitely not my style."

"If they're close enough to stab, they're close enough to shoot," Solace said, patting one of the two laser pistols holstered and slung low on her hips. "I say we land on yonder rise, and scope out the situation. Maybe we can spot the men before the battle starts."

**** 

Hidden beneath a cottonwood, Malachi closed his eyes, and put his other senses on high alert. Scenes from last evening's interlude with Port grabbed him by the bollocks, and he sucked in a deep breath.

She had surrendered her body to him—and almost all of her heart. Afterward, they had talked about many things. Little by little, he seemed to be gaining back her trust. He could control her emotions by using magic, casting spells until what earthlings called the cows came home, but he didn't want her under false pretenses.

It had surprised him when she revealed her thoughts about going back to their previous occupation with the SCI. Space Counter Intelligence had been fun and exciting, but a young man's sport. He had no intention of spending the rest of their hopefully long life together gallivanting across the Multiverse dodging deadly situations while battling brutal creatures like Thurax. Although, truth be told, he looked forward to facing that miserable brute today.

Reconnecting with Portence prior to all out combat had been the best of occurrences in the worst of circumstances. He wanted to woo his warrior woman, emphasis on the woman aspect. Take all the time they wanted—and never had. Learn about and enjoy one another at their leisure. Again he realized how much the adrenalin rush of special ops, and gallivanting around the Multiverse, had lost its appeal. He could go for a big dose of tranquility.

His senses quickened when he detected someone

approaching. Determining it was Tanner, he kept his eyes closed.

"You shouldn't be daydreaming," the ex-Army Ranger chided. "I could have slit your throat."

Malachi opened his eyes, and smiled. "I heard you coming a hundred yards away. But I appreciate your concern." He liked Tanner, a brave warrior, and from what he could tell, an honorable man.

The big soldier gave a bark of amusement. "Lawson has gone over the hill to round up some of his crew. They're relocating a makeshift emergency center closer to where today's action should take place."

"Sounds like a smart move. Hand to hand can get messy."

"Wish we knew what weapons this Hephaestus guy hammered together for the Reps."

"Whatever it is, it will probably involve fire."

"Sounds pretty short range."

"Guided by magic."

"Oh…damn. That puts a different spin on things. I'm not used to dealing with all this mystical mumbo-jumbo."

This time Malachi gave a chuckle. "At least now you have magic on your side too."

"And glad of it."

"Nate's here."

Tanner glanced around then back the way he'd come. "I don't see him."

"You will."

Moments later, their brainiac friend, appeared wending his way through the stand of trees. "Glad the fog's lifting," he said, coming to a halt.

"You're just in time," Malachi said. "The Fae are

here too." He nodded toward the three female warriors as they appeared beneath a ledge on the far ridge.

They stood tall, side by side, metallic battle wings overlapping like a shield-wall at their back. Red, black, and white respectively, their hair fluttered in the low breeze, the effect surreal, lending a delicate quality to the image, masking the strength he knew each one possessed.

"Lord above, they are magnificent," Nate murmured.

"Indeed," Malachi said. His heartbeat quickened at the sight of his woman, the last wisps of fog swirling at her feet as she stood in command of all she surveyed.

Tanner raised the binoculars hanging around his neck to study them more closely. "They look well-armed and good to go. Did you get the laser rechargers moved closer," he asked Nate.

"You bet. Don't want the ladies running on empty. Sorry I couldn't make shotguns for everyone, but Mother nixed the idea. Some cosmic rule about not endowing humans with galactic weaponry. I of course being the exception to the rule."

Malachi smiled, Mother seemed to have a keen attraction for the human cowboy. No doubt something to do with the allure of the Old West and its heroes.

"My men are better off using firepower they're accustomed to." Tanner assured. "They're locked and loaded, and waiting for my signal to advance. And even outnumbered as we are, we can still take 'em."

"That's what I like to hear." Nate nodded. "I'm going airborne. I think you'll enjoy what I've worked up. It's steampunk meets Buck Rogers." Turning he jogged back the way he'd come.

For one fleeting moment, Malachi wondered how it had all come about. Never in a millennium would he have thought to be about to go into battle against a horde of Reptiles with only three Fae Warriors, and a handful of humans. He was up for a good fight, of course. Still it seemed so primitive, this close-in combat, yet natural, he supposed, and inbred and instinctual in the male entity. It was how every species began, and how many species ended.

****

Port felt his presence down below, just as she knew Malachi could feel her energy. Thoughts of love replaced those of war—until she spotted Xandora.

"Jumping Jupiter," Bliss said, pointing as if anyone could miss the spectacle.

"What in the name of Hypnos is she aloft in?" Solace asked.

"Looks like a canopy bed, rigged-out for a thirteen-year-old female Hume." Port could barely believe her eyes as the profusion of pink ruffles hovered off the ground near the center of the enemy camp. It had a haziness about it indicating a protection spell—Malachi's or Hephaestus'? She knew Mother had snookered Malachi into babysitting the brat. She supposed it hardly mattered. If it was his, he could break it. If it was Heph's, Malachi could still break it.

Xandora stood tall at the foot of the bed, holding onto one wooden post supporting the canopy. Working her mouth as if shouting orders, she suddenly flung wide her other arm. When she did, the beating of many drums erupted. The sound, deep and dirge-like, split the cold silence.

It had begun.

With a whoop and a holler, all three sisters took to the air.

The Reps, surprisingly organized, quickly filed through the narrow gap separating their camp from the battlefield. Thurax, easy to spot with his glowing green hair, led the first group of Reps as they spread out to meet the soldiers on the level field.

Tanner's men waited on this side of the valley.

The Reps were accustomed to overwhelming their enemies with brute strength, their willingness to die like Viking berserkers a terrifying weapon in itself. They stood side by side, six Reps deep, unclothed from the waist up. The camo fatigue pants they did wear blended together making them appear as one huge creature with hundreds of arms and heads. Scaly heads—which they thrust into the air as they roared and snapped their jaws. Along with new side arms, each carried a spear, the tip raised skyward. As they jockeyed for position, morning sun glinted off the forest of metal points.

The Reps made the first move.

"Fire balls," Bliss warned, as one came directly at her. She blasted it out of the air with her laser shot gun.

Because they knew Malachi could warp the trajectory of regular bullets, Hephaestus had relied on what he knew best, adding his own touch of magic. Thankfully the weapon's range was limited, but when a fiery projectile did reach a target, the results were devastating.

The E.T. Squad and Army backup troops were dressed to the teeth, wearing experimental equipment beyond state-of-the-art. The hail of fire hindered them little, and they kept advancing at a steady pace. Their plan for today—down and dirty, no holds barred—as they pushed the enemy back. They also needed to contain and detain. The enemy had enough men to try circling around to outflank them, or to come up from the rear. Heck, once out of their canyon enclave, the Reps could end up anywhere, even back in town.

Some of the U.S. Army bullets reached the Reptiles, but some didn't. Port figured Gorlock had tried and partially succeeded in replicating Malachi's projectile bending spell. Regardless, based on the gag-worthy odor hanging over the valley, plenty of Reps were wounded if not dead.

There were wounded good guys, too. The healthy shuttled the injured off the field on stretchers. Lance would soon have his hands full.

A fireball clipped the edge of one of Port's wings, doing little damage, but greatly ticking her off. Since the enemy appeared enamored with flaming objects, turnabout seemed fair play.

Returning to the ridge, arms extended to the heavens, Port chanted the prayer of making she learned as a child. "Fire, spirit of the south, come to me now. Lend us your help. As you give us your energy, in return we give you the fire of love and devotion. Your spirit is keeper of the hearth and the eternal flame. Listen to me now and bend to my will."

She swayed in rhythm with the earth, her hair swirling and haloing around her. Vibrations filled the air, then her body. She raised her left arm, hand out, palm up. Sparks of electricity began to rise. By command they clustered and floated before her.

A bit of ball lightning sounded just the thing. Simpler to create than some of her more extreme makings, and less likely to go awry. Besides, it never hurt to limber up and get in the swing of things when you were dealing with a bazillion volts of electricity.

The glowing sphere wavered back and forth, shifting from silver to gold, pulsing like a living being as it grew stronger. Invisibly connected, it crackled and hummed, sending jolts through her with a heady rush.

Harnessing her gift didn't always come easy, but was usually spectacular. On special ops, she'd used it plenty of times, but she'd had Malachi at her side back then. He'd lent a hand pinpointing targets and containing the rare chain reactions she'd inadvertently created. He'd been there in so many ways. Just the two of them against the Multiverse. That's how it had felt. Like they could conquer anything, as long as they were together. Athena, please watch over him. Indelibly part of her past, she now realized Malachi was also undeniably part of her future. He was the one to share her life's journey.

As her desire for him raced through her body, the ball of fire soaked up the energy, gaining power in leaps and bounds. She chanted once more, giving it her all, the act of creating leaving her wild with exhilaration.

The globe of fire fought to break free, spitting off bits of electricity like an angry cat, but she stayed strong, commanding it do her bidding, telling it what target she sought. Then she cast wide her arms sending the enormous circle of lightning hurtling across the valley.

Tearing up the earth like a meteor impact, her *weapon* sent dirt, rock, and bushes tumbling into the air. Gravity returned the debris, raining it down on the gnarly lizard heads. Stunned, the enemy troops stopped in their web-footed tracks.

The landscape remained wet from the recent rain, helping to prevent a grass fire, and the smoldering damp flora kicked up some nice dark smoke. Taking note, Solace, sent a breeze to blow the billowing haze away from their position and toward the Reps. The enemy retreated, halting just short of the mouth to the pass. Their movements were disorganized, accompanied by the sounds of fear, pain, and coughing. The E.T. Squad captured the few stragglers left behind.

She'd foiled the first wave of attack, but it wouldn't stop them for long. At least her side could use the time to regroup too. They'd pushed the enemy back, which had to instill confidence, and prove to the Humes even an alien Reptile wasn't invincible. Still, her team remained severely outnumbered. If they could whittle them down bit by bit, they might have a chance.

## Chapter Sixteen

Port glanced around for Xandora.

The mad sub-goddess, still aloft in her canopied cradle, screamed like an enraged child. Cheeks red from exertion, she flailed about with such fury she lost her balance and tumbled backward amidst the mound of pillows.

Too big of a temptation to resist, Port took to the air. With a gentle flap of her wings, she hung motionless a short distance away from the wretched creature. The entity responsible for this chaos, pain, and suffering didn't look very pretty with her face twisted in anger.

"Having a rough day," Port called over to her.

"I hate you," Xandora shrieked, struggling up onto her knees. "You and your stupid sisters. You're ruining everything." She grasped a spear lying on the bed. Another gift from Heph? Xandy touched the end, and it burst into flame confirming Port's suspicions. The prissy little princess chucked the flaming spear with surprising strength and accuracy.

Before she could flash-move out of the way, Malachi shoved her aside, catching the spear midair with his other hand. Horror for what had nearly happened darkened his expression. Then it turned deadly. He hurtled the spear back the way it had come.

The business end of the flaming shaft imbedded

deep into the headboard, rather than in Xandora's heaving chest.

"You missed," Port said, knowing full well he'd hit exactly what he'd aimed for.

"Mother bade me watch over the wrathful creature, but as she just tried to kill you, being bound to such a promise is becoming rather a conundrum.

Xandora stared at the spear shaft still vibrating back and forth, then at the two of them. In an instant, her expression jumped from wide-eyed surprise, to wolf-snarling animosity.

"Mind the fire, dear heart," Malachi said, indicating she should look behind her.

With a yelp of fear rather than anger, Xandora scrambled across the bed on hands and knees, slapping at the burning headboard. A wave of Malachi's hand sent the memory foam chariot spinning off toward the enemy camp, back to the dark side Xandora had chosen to call her own.

"She's really going to be pissed now," Port said.

"She's perfected the skill. I believe when she was created, her first thought was of revenge."

Port glanced around for her sisters. Solace was busy blasting away at a small band of leftover Hover Rats. The attack appeared to be a last ditch effort. After a few casualties, the bedraggled avian rat-faces again turned tail and ran—and not back toward the enemy camp. This time, they were out of here for good.

Farther to the west, Bliss and Noodge made ready to intercept a Rep who hadn't retreated with the others. Good job Bliss. He was AWOL and heading toward the new triage base. A rogue Rep spelled trouble, he'd be out for survival, with only killing on its mind.

Gaining altitude, Port and Malachi hung aloft side by side. "Looks to me like even more reinforcements arrived during the night," she said, watching as Thurax rallied his troops.

"But look," Malachi pointed out. "They're having to reload already. Quite a drawback. Heph's fireballs are a passably good idea, but too antiquated. The Reps won't fight for long with inferior weapons."

"What if we drove them back into the canyon? We could block off the pass leading from the camp to valley, and keep them contained. Maybe even force a surrender."

"But if we have to eventually go in after them," he countered, "fighting in close quarters will be even more dangerous."

"Maybe rather than going in, the E.T. Squad and Civilian Army soldier could gain cover in the far hills surrounding the canyon."

"They could, but I'm guessing they won't. They'll want to be in the thick of it. Better bounce it off Tanner. The men are his responsibility."

They landed, and Port followed through with the suggestion. She pressed her handheld against one ear to block the wind noise, but her efforts to concentrate faltered as Malachi slid one hand around her waist, kissing her neck just below her other ear.

"Are you sure? Okay, you got it." She tucked the communicator away, and gently pushed against Malachi's chest interrupting the rather delightful teasing.

"What'd Tanner say?" he asked, giving her one last nuzzle.

"He liked the idea of containment within the

canyon. But there'll be no holding back. If we eventually go in, so does the E.T. Squad. He reassured me this is what they've trained for."

"Brave…and hopefully not as foolish as it sounds."

As if someone had sounded a signal, both sides suddenly squared off and raced toward one another again. The air filled with the terrible sound of warfare as the two forces met on the slopes of the valley.

Solace and Bliss rushed over, laser shotguns at the ready, and the four of them went airborne above what soon became a melee in the truest sense. Noodge stood on the outskirts of the free-for-all, catching any Rep striking out on his own.

"They're so bunched up I can't get a clear shot," Solace said. Daring to swoop in closer, she isolated a few targets and blasted away.

By sheer numbers and muscle power the Humes were outnumbered, and it began to show. More and more soldiers were being wounded.

"We better do something and soon," Bliss warned. "And where do you suppose Nate is?"

Port stopped firing to answer. "When I spoke to Tanner, about closing the pass, he said Nate had a temporary malfunction with one of the crystals Mother gave him. But he'll be here soon."

"How about another little breeze to help things along?" Solace offered, returning to their side. She raised her arms, calling, "Air Spirit of the East, I ask you once again to answer my call. Look into my heart—we are grateful. Now for the good of all, it needs be done." Currents of air swirled madly, dancing about as to an unheard tune. Then the power coalesced, seemly waiting for her command. "Blow the beast back to his lair, blow hard, blow now."

With a great roar, the wind swooped down across the valley, a trail of debris churning in its wake. Reps and Humes alike tumble and rolled across the battle field. Having nowhere to go, the Humes hunkered down. Scrambling and scratching, the Reps made their way to the passage, and back through it to the safety of the camp.

"Do your thing, sis," Bliss said.

With Malachi close behind her, Port flash-moved and set down about a hundred yards from the rock pathway through which the Reps had made their escape.

"Mind if I do the honors?" she asked, still in the mood for creating with fire.

He gave a gentlemanly bow, and extended his hand in the direction of the high-walled pass. "Always a pleasure watching you work. But don't exhaust yourself. I have pleasures of another nature in mind for you later."

*Hurry sundown.*

Malachi stood at her shoulder, not interfering, yet ready to help. What she planned this time went beyond her prior bit of making. Setting free her inner strength, she drew down power from beyond the Earth's atmosphere. Time slowed, and where she stood became an illusion.

Again offering gratitude for her gift, she allowed the cosmic energy to race through her body, as she embraced the pleasure/pain fighting for control. Just like the wind Solace could conjure, the elements had their own lives, and the lightning longed for freedom. The natural forces came to us not so much unwillingly, but with expectations. To make energy cost energy. Light shot from her fingertips, high into the air, now with purpose and pattern. Too bright to look upon, she saw the entity of fire and light with her mind's eye. Dazzling, beautiful, deadly.

"Element of earth, gird your spirit, for at my bidding, this formation shall be transformed."

She released the pillar of fire. Unrestrained, the bolt burst forth, and traveling at the speed of light, the flash broke the sound barrier. Thunder rolled across the valley adding to the cataclysm—and the fun. The earth reverberated as the target imploded. Rocks fractured and tumbled. The passage was sealed.

The three sisters and Malachi stood nearby, waiting for the dust to settle. Down in the valley, the soldiers regrouped, the healthy helped the wounded to the transports waiting to take the injured to Lance. When Port spotted Captain Jackson looking their way, she nudged Solace and pointed. Her sister breathed a sigh of relief and waved down at her partner.

"Look," Bliss said, gazing skyward.

Nate was here now too. He and his balloon, hung in the air, drifting closer.

"With the Reps holed-up in there, we should give them a chance to surrender," Bliss suggested.

Fair-play ranked high on her sister's personal code of ethic. Port leaned more toward *ya pay's your money, and you takes your chances.* Or *war is hell, and now you're in it.* "I suppose it can't hurt to ask if they want to white-flag-it, but the answer seems rather obvious."

"Not the point," Bliss persisted. "It's a matter of conscience and cosmic justice, and we'll have given them a chance to make things right."

"I agree," Solace put in. "You're accustomed to special ops, last ditch efforts with no viable alternatives. This is the real Multiverse, where we're supposed to try and get along. Or as these Humes would say, uphold truth, justice, and the American way."

Sarcasm flavored Solace's words as if she knew getting along with a Rep meant ending up dead. Still, Port admired the integrity shown by both her sisters. And if by some long shot they did surrender, it could save many Hume lives.

"Far be it from me," she relented, "to tarnish the reputation of the Sisters of Anu."

Noodge howled in agreement.

"So whom do we send on this deadly mission of goodwill?" she asked.

When Malachi stepped forward, her heart faltered. She knew it was the most logical choice, but the idea made her wingports twitch, and not in a good way. Why did he have to be so noble?

"Got some loose ends to tie up anyway," he said.

What did he mean? Xandora, Thurax, Gorlock? This made her worry all the more.

"Loose ends my asteroid. You can get your payback-fix when we all go in. Just get the message to them as safely as possible, and when they refuse, come back to me in one piece."

"You do care," he said, with a half-smile, making light of her words. But the flash of light in tawny yellow eyes indicated deeper emotion.

Port liberated a five-foot atlatl dart from the back-quiver she wore. The wooden shaft, used for war would now be used for improbable peace. "Anybody got some white fabric?"

Bliss rummaged in the mini-tote attached to her woven canvas belt. When she came up with an embroidered white linen handkerchief, hoots of much needed laughter broke out. Only Bliss would carry such a frilly item into battle, and only Malachi would be masculine enough to pull off waiving it at a Rep.

Quickly attaching it, Port handed the shaft to him. "This should get you close enough to negotiate. If they balk at talking or show any signs of aggression promise you'll get the heck out of there. Play it safe."

His smile grew, filled with warmth. "It's not my style, but for you, I'll try."

Striding closer to the rock wall, as if he hadn't a care in the world, Malachi set out. By walking rather than flying or flash-moving, it allowed the enemy time to consider his non-threatening approach.

The Reps peered down from the stony ledges now holding them prisoners. They brandished their weapons, but made no threatening moves. When Malachi came within shouting distance, he halted and raised the white flag. An exchange of words appeared to follow. Again, when no form of retaliation ensued, she breathed a little easier. Then one Rep threw a rope ladder over the rocky ridge.

Malachi advanced, took hold of the hemp, and began to climb. What was he doing? *Just deliver the message and leave.* The words screamed through her mind with such force she knew he could hear her, but he didn't alter course. He was going inside.

Frick.

She should never have let him go, at least not alone.

****

Portence's ire pommeled him like a physical sensation. But there was no turning back—even if he wanted to—which he didn't. Unobtrusively using his power of levitation, he swiftly ascended the ladder. Reaching the top, he forced himself to stand calmly as a Rep snatched the *flag* from his hand, and a second scaly ruffian patted him down for weapons which seemed quite silly since his most powerful armament was his mind.

"I've a message for Xandora," he stated.

"I'm guessing she has a few words for you as well, traitor." The Rep with the atlatl dart grinned, and then nodded for him to precede down the far side of the escarpment. He hadn't taken three steps toward the heart of the activity before he felt the pointy end of the dart poking him, none too gently, in the back.

Reptiles of varying sizes stepped aside jeering and growling as he passed by. One even shoved at his shoulder making him stumble. Resisting the urge to retaliate, or to put up a shield, he walked on. As he'd kept watch over Xandora, he'd sheltered with these entities for days on end, but he'd interacted with them as little as possible. None of them, not even Gorlock, knew his true capabilities, and a show of vulnerability would keep them off their guard until he assessed the situation.

He doubted Thurax or Xandora would surrender, which meant a full-out battle awaited all of them. His comrades, Fae, and both furry and Hume, would fight to the end, and being available on the inside seemed the best advantage he could give them.

When they reached a large tented structure, on the outskirts of the main activity, they halted. A weak and sloppily constructed protection spell surrounded the habitat, Gorlock's doing no doubt. He gave a snort of derision at the amateurish attempt, and dissolved it.

The Rep Commander known as Botu pulled aside the tent door, then gave him a vigorous shove through the opening. Sidestepping to gained his balance, he glanced around. As his eyes adjusted to the dim light, the triumvirate shimmered into view. It was really too much.

Upon a raised dais, sat Thurax, Xandora, and Hephaestus—the Queen in the middle, flanked by her warrior on the right, and her mentor on the left. Gorlock, buffoon extraordinaire, stood in the background, a jester at their beck and call.

Xandora rose gracefully, and descended the steps, her limp barely noticeable as she strode forward to stand before him.

"I knew you couldn't stay away from me for long," she smiled coquettishly. Then she slapped him across the face. "But I shan't forgive you so easily."

He gritted his teeth against the unexpected blow, yet what came as an even bigger surprise was the misguided fact she thought he'd come back because of amorous intentions. Xandora's fantasies knew now bounds.

"I told you the turncoat left here hand in hand with the Fae," Thurax cruelly pointed out, his voice booming down from where he remained seated. "Somehow I doubt love is the emotion driving him back into your arms."

Xandora's body stiffened, and her brown eyes deepened to near black. Malachi knew the thinnest of tethers held back blind rage.

"But I do care what happens to you, Xandora," he placated. "In fact it's why I'm here. I've been asked to negotiate peaceful terms of surrender."

Her shoulders relaxed, and a thoughtful expression crossed her face. "I'm glad your side has finally come to their senses," she said brightly. "We accept, and shall be merciful to all whom we take prisoner."

"Not our surrender—yours."

Laughter filled the room.

"Why on this pitiful Earth would I surrender? I've just learned we've killed three Fae warriors yesterday in outlying areas."

*Might have been good knowing this going in. The sisters would be deeply saddened by this news.*

"I can see by your poorly masked surprise you were unaware of our victory. Yes, two of the nasty creatures died in the California territory, and one in the city called Chicago."

"There's a great difference between winning a few battles and winning the war. Besides, those two areas are the only ones where you still hold sway. Globally you're done. This is your last stand, Xandora, and you're on shaky ground."

Thurax gave a sneer of derision from where he sat. Then unfolding his huge form, he stretched to his full height, and stared down at the two of them as if they were both becoming unworthy of his tolerance. His green hair had been braided and adorned with copper beads—Xandora's influence no doubt. But he still dressed like a barbarian beneath the silk cape. It would take more than a new hair style and a little bling to civilize such a brute.

"Why are you really here, sorcerer?" Thurax

descended the stairs of the dais. "Surrender is not in my DNA, nor in theirs." He nodded toward the Reptile commander where he stood just inside the door. "I doubt it is in yours either. Which leaves us with a grave problem."

Always seeking the spotlight, Gorlock rushed forward to join in the trash talking. "No telling what's in this cross/breed's DNA. I'll not surrender either."

Malachi bit back his first response, then said, "There would be no need for your surrender, Gorlock. Just as there would be no need for the surrender of that field mouse over there, or the birds in the trees. You are of no significance."

Botu gave an ungodly reptile laugh. Gorlock became apoplectic as he retrieved a wand from an inner pocket in his robe.

Rather than create a shield around himself, Malachi threw up a containment spell around Gorlock, rendering him harmless. Then he faced Thurax, the one enemy on this planet he could count on who wanted him dead the most. Whether Xandora wanted him alive or not seemed to be a tossup.

She stepped sideways, and gingerly placed one hand on Thurax's forearm. The idea of touching him didn't seem to come easily. "If victory is not to be ours," she said, showing fear of defeat for the first time, "could we not just call it quits."

Malachi felt a flash of disbelief for the childish woman. She viewed masterminding death and destruction on a planetary scale as simple delinquent behavior. Now she was ready to stop and say sorry.

"When the choice is surrender or death," Thurax snarled, "death *is* victory."

With a look of desperation, Xandora quickly withdrew her hand, and turned toward Hephaestus.

"I'm immortal," he tossed down from the dais, with a jolly laugh. "It's all the same to me."

"Shut up you old fool," Thurax ordered. "You have been of little help. Your ways are of the past, we are the future."

"The time grows short for your answer," Malachi said.

"What are you talking about?" Xandora said, ringing her hands. "You mean we have to decide this very minute."

"Yes. They'll be no lingering siege tactics. The deadline for a decision is now."

"We fight." Thurax shook his fist in the air.

Botu returned the gesture, and with a growl, he took a step closer to Malachi.

Gorlock threw down sparks and smoke. The containment spell kept the murky air in place growing thicker by the moment, leaving the hackneyed magician sputtering and coughing.

"Is this your answer as well?" Malachi directed the question to Xandora, giving her every possible chance to surrender. She had been at odds with the Multiverse since day one, perhaps it just wasn't in her to change. He held out his hand. She shook her head no.

"I shall deliver your answer," Malachi said.

"You shall deliver nothing," Thurax countered. "When you don't return, they'll get the idea."

## Chapter Seventeen

Port stood in the indecisive sunlight, reminding herself to breathe. The dust from the skirmishes, the windstorm, and the collapse of the tunnel had long settled, and it was eerily silent.

Solace placed one hand on Port's shoulder to get her attention. In her other hand, Solace clasped her handheld. "We're past the agreed deadline for an answer, and Tanner's asking for an update on Malachi's situation. What should I tell him?"

"They won't let him walk out of there," Port said, fighting to keep the panic restricted to her mind, and not her voice. "And with tons of volcanic rock between us, I can't feel him. He's either dead or waiting for us to attack."

Bliss stepped up, offering her superior skills, and eyes closed she reached out toward the war headquarters of their enemy. "A small spot of good energy exists amongst the evil. He's waiting." Eyes open she smiled at Port.

"Then let's go get him." Port knew if she switched to warrior mode, survival would be her only concern, automatically forcing the fear, anger, and anxiety to become secondary. It might be the only way she was going to get through this. "Tell Tanner we're going in."

"Wait," Bliss said, countermanding the order. "I hear a noise."

Fae ears on alert, a gentle whirring caught their attention.

"It's Nate," Bliss said, pointing.

His hot air balloon hovered in the sky, high enough to avoid the fire balls, but close enough for them to see him clearly. With his cowboy hat pulled low, and a laser shotgun slung across his back, he worked with the newly installed equipment.

"Looks like he perfected his EMP apparatus," Bliss said, with a big smile for the Hume she loved. "Now things are gonna heat up, especially some Reptile backsides."

The humming grew louder, and a wave of electromagnetic heat began to emanate from the basket beneath the balloon. Rippling and fanning outward, it blanketed the Rep camp like a high riding cloud of crystal clear water.

Noodge cocked his head and whined. The three sisters stared in fascination, and then took to the air to watch from above.

As the undulating cloud throbbed and shimmered, all the creatures directly below began slapping at their bodies and running to and fro.

The EMP rays didn't seem selective. Port let out a cry of concern. "Hey, doesn't he know Malachi is down there too?"

**** 

Thurax and Botu ran from the tent to see what was happening. Malachi conjured wings, and followed suit, ready to take flight. Then the tips of his wings caught fire. Son of a bitch that hurt, he dematerialized them. While his Fae abilities seemed to work, his power as a sorcerer did not. It must be the EMP?

168

As chaos ensued, the Reptiles appeared to be in the greatest distress, their unprotected lizard skin sizzling as they ran yelping in pain, snarling and snapping at one another. Malachi's containment spell now gone, Gorlock's robes began to smolder, as did Thurax's green hair. Heading in the opposite direction, Xandora and Hephaestus ran up along the canyon wall. Protected by an overhang, they watched from afar.

Mysterious and pulsing, the cloud shifted about in a random pattern, offering no option for circumventing the heat and irritating sensation raining down on them. Malachi had known the chances of getting caught in some kind of crossfire had been high, but it was easier dodging bullets than a friggin' death ray. He also knew he was expendable, and Tanner and Nate would do whatever was necessary to end this conflict.

"You should have surrendered," he called to Thurax.

His nemesis snarled, took a running start, and head down, plowed into Malachi. Both crashed to the ground. His magic still eluded him, but then there was something to be said for the unadulterated satisfaction of smashing one's fist into an enemy's face. Drawing now on his Fae abilities, he grappled and wailed away, giving as good as he got.

Strong as a Taurus Trader's bull, Thurax took blow after blow with little effect. But being bigger left him slower, and many of his strikes were easily avoided, glancing off, not doing much damage.

As the heat from above amplified, Malachi shed his long coat, the protection now becoming cumbersome. Already stripped down to bare necessities, sweat poured off of Thurax. Having come from a cold planet, the importance of heat tolerance apparently ranked low in the evolution of his species.

The sauna effect didn't thrill Malachi much either. He needed to get out of here and back to Portence. But first things first.

Recalling the pain and loss she had endured because of the soulless being he faced—and because of his own decisions—rage sparked in every cell in Malachi's body. Even a little magic burst free, and he roared like the tiger he felt seething within. Startled, Thurax took several steps back. Pursuing the advantage, Malachi ran forward, ending with a roundhouse kick that left the green haired bastard teetering on the edge of the nearby ravine.

Dressed in regulation gear, Botu seemed less affected by the heat ray than his shirtless Reptile buddies. When he lumbered forward, Malachi didn't wait to find out if the big Reptile held out a hand to Thurax, or gave him a boot over the edge.

Again calling upon his Fae abilities, Malachi took to the air. This time using nonflammable metal wings, he leaped upward, fighting his way into the miasma.

The heat increased to a near fatal degree, and fighting to gain altitude felt like crawling through molten honey while being dragged over a torturous washboard. The semiliquid atmosphere precluded breathing, leaving his lungs screaming for air. Slowing his heartbeat helped to ease the panic, and using intuition to guide his path, he headed for the far edge of what felt like eternity.

After all the times he'd cheated death, he never imagined this was the way he would die. Then he felt her, and he knew all would be well. He grabbed the hand Portence extended, and she pulled him the rest of the way out. Exhausted and gasping for a decent breath, he hung in place, barely flapping metal wings now nearing meltdown temperature.

"You're as hot as the re-entry panel of our old ship," she said, urging him higher and higher, where the air was thinner, but also much cooler.

She gently smoothed the hair back from his bruised and battered face, and the expression in her eyes spoke of concern, but also of love. Lips met, and the kiss stole his breath—this time in a good way. Cooling down from the EMP ray, he heated up in other areas, making him want more than just a kiss. Too bad this was neither the time nor place. Holding on to one another, they slowly turned around and around, and losing altitude with each rotation they gently touched down.

Solace and Bliss landed beside them.

"Ladies," Malachi acknowledged, releasing his hold on Portence. "This clever heat ray might give us a second shot at trying surrender negotiations. I dare say the fight is out of them by now."

"No way," Port insisted, leaning ever so slightly against him. "You're not going back in there a second time—at least not alone.

As inconspicuously as possible, he reached for her hand.

"We can only hope Nate's non-lethal weapon will eventually convince them to give up the fight," Bliss agreed.

"If not, Tanner's team is ready to storm the canyon," Solace added. "But it won't be a pretty sight if we have to go into that pit after those scaly-ass Reps."

All gazes turned toward the enemy camp.

****

Xandora paced along the edge of the cliff cave, trying not to get too close to the dirty walls. Thank goodness Hephaestus had gotten her out of camp before that horrid cloud took effect.

All of a sudden, as if it had short-circuited, the veil overhead blinked and went out.

Quick to make use of the opportunity, Thurax stormed out of the melee and up a nearby path on the canyon wall. Commander Botu, clamored along behind him. Gorlock, the silly goose, brought up the rear, waving his wand and flapping his arms. Scrambling sideways along the ridge, Xandora sought to intercept them, and to find out what they intended to do about this situation.

"What's going on?" she demanded, stepping onto the trail they followed. "Why are you up here instead of leading my troops to victory?"

"You stupid woman," Thurax snarled, as the cloud blinked back on, pouring out heat once again. "Your troops are being fried alive."

"Don't you dare speak to me like that," she snapped back, glaring at the nasty beast. "And where is Malachi? I saw you fighting with him, even after I asked you not to cross horns with him."

Thurax raised a fist and loomed closer. He dared to sniff at her as if he were a dog detecting something rotten. Then an odd expression crossed his ugly face. He took a step back nearly crashing into Botu. That was better. Who did Thurax think he was talking to her in such manner? He was hired help.

"Your golden-eyed magician is gone once more," he said, with a sneer of satisfaction. "We should have killed the redheaded Fae when we had the chance, and burned the sorcerer at the stake. He's double crossed you twice now. This time with the help of the white-haired Fae Warrior."

The blood drained from her head, and she grabbed a nearby boulder to keep upright. He was lying. "How do you know this?" she demanded, searching the sky for signs of her lover.

"I watched them fly away together—hand in hand."

"I saw them too," Botu growled.

"Don't look so surprised. You're the one who welcomed the traitor back with open arms," Thurax reminded. "Him and his insulting request of surrender."

Could it be true? She saw now Malachi was in league with the Fae. That meant Mother was in on this too. But Malachi had previously put the spell of keeping on her. Thurax had just felt it. Had Malachi done so out of true concern for her, or at Mother's command? Fury, hotter than Vesuvius in its heyday, raced through her veins, and her body shook with rage. How was it she didn't explode from the heat and pressure?

"Damn you, Malachi, to the center ring of Hades' circus." She truly, just about, almost, well pretty much, thought she loved him—and yet he betrayed her.

In a blind rage, she paced about not even caring when her beautiful dress snagged on a bush, and dust covered her shoes. Everything was falling apart.

Thurax shoved Botu aside, and started up the hill behind where they stood. What was he up to now? The only thing of import up there was the dam. She opened her mouth to demand he return to her side. Instead, she held her words and smiled. So be it. What better time to use the mightiest weapon in her repertoire.

Raising the hem of her torn frock, she scrambled up the incline after him. Botu trudged along several yards behind. He might be formidable on flat land, but he seemed out of his element on an incline. And what was he hollering about? She couldn't understand a word he said, and she certainly wasn't about to turn back to find out what had him such a tizzy.

The plastic explosives had been set days ago. A single push of a button was all it would take. Oh, this was going to be so much fun. She'd show the puny humans, and Mother's favorite fawning Fae creatures a thing or two. After which, she intended to put Thurax in his place. He assumed too much.

Standing a safe distance above the dam, she watched with glee.

"This should cool down the troops." Thurax laughed, grabbing up the detonator.

Commander Botu finally caught up with them—out of breath and still loudly yammering on about something. Anger and fear enlivened his words as he rudely shoved her out of the way and barreled into Thurax. The green-haired mercenary, one of the few entities equal in strength to the Rep, deftly rolled to one side and gained his feet. Not waiting for a second attack, he set off the charges.

A quiet rumbling could be heard and felt deep in the earth. Then it grew louder and louder, and the ground exploded upward, launching rocks in every direction. Fighting to remain upright, Xandora hid as best she could.

Water trickled through the small cracks in the dam,

slowly at first, then the cracks widened and the wall crumbled, chunk by huge chunk, releasing an unstoppable torrent. Tearing away more pieces of foundation, it thrashed and churned, picking up dirt and debris as it rushed down the mountainside, heading toward the camp and the town down below.

Commander Botu raged on, wrestling Thurax to the ground, and they battled like two Titans of old.

"What the hell's the matter with you," Thurax ground out, between blows given and received.

Botu wrapped his clawed fingers around Thurax's throat and roared. "You idiot, my species can't swim."

Chapter Eighteen

Soldier's instinct or good old human intuition? Either way, Tanner turned and glanced at the top of the mountain just as the sound of the explosion reached him. Dirt and rock pitched into the air, and fearing the worst, he grabbed the walkie-talkie.

"Platoon leaders, fall back," he ordered. "They blew the dam. Relocate all personnel to higher ground. Over." Each response came back roger/copy that.

Holding ready to take over the enemy camp, two platoons were positioned in the surrounding hills. His third platoon patrolled Colorado Springs in case the Reps got out and made another try for the town. They too were ordered to seek higher ground, hunker down, and wait.

Where was Nate, he wondered searching the sky? His friend had discontinued the airborne attack, and moved the balloon farther away. *Good thinking, buddy. And thanks.* The EMP ray had bought them valuable time, delaying the need for military interaction and the chance of higher casualties. The Reps, visible in the canyon, appeared confused by the sudden silence, and the withdrawal of the heat ray. The reason was on its way.

A dull roar preceded the water as it tore along, ripping trees up by the roots and dislodging boulders the size of cars—the dam may have been a tad deeper than estimated. Slow to respond, the Reptiles were caught in the avalanche of water, and fighting for their lives, they were washed out of the canyon and down the mountainside.

"Give me an update, Charlie leader? Use the micro-vid-cam. I need to know what's going on down there."

Thanks to Nate, each platoon leader now had a miniature video camera attached to their combat helmets, the devise rested at eye level, and the accompanying wrist screen Tanner wore, allowed him to see what they saw. Using satellite transmission, the range pushed all limits.

"We are secure and on high ground, Captain," came the response. "Rousted and detained two noncombatants who had returned after the initial evacuation. We are one klick east of the town. Over."

Tanner watched a soldier hustle the civilians out of view. "Hold your ground. The water is almost to your sector."

"Holy crap, sir. I see it coming now. They weren't kidding, Captain, when they said those buggers can't swim. Over."

"A break for us," Tanner acknowledged. "I have your visual."

The screen depicted the wall of water carrying the floundering Reptiles. As it inundated the town, the Reps smashed into buildings and through plate glass windows like scaly green wrecking balls.

There went an electrical pole. It toppled sideways—the wires snapping and sending sparks flying through the air. A second wave of water lifted a delivery truck, flinging it into a pump at the service station. The dislodged nozzle leaked gasoline, and the oily liquid, floating on top of the water, burst into flame as the downed power line made contact. The miniature image he watched could be a trailer for the latest Armageddon movie.

Tough and resilient, several Reps survived being half-drowned, hurled down the mountainside, and scorched in the gasoline fire—and one was too many. Running amuck, they stormed about smashing through whatever stood in their way.

"Charlie platoon, engage enemy at will, and contain that fire," Tanner ordered.

The mini-cam showed a pitched battle, with close contact. Then he lost visual, but he could hear the bursts of gunfire echo up from below as the battle continued. After several tense moments, silence reigned.

"Charlie platoon, situation report. Over."

"Enemy engaged and eliminated. We have no dead, but five wounded, three seriously. The fire is under control. Over."

"Are you in a defensible position now?"

"Roger that. We are secure, sir.

"Select a transport team and take the injured to Fountain City, their hospital is still functional. Over."

"Roger that."

"Good luck, over and out."

Knowing his men were as safe as possible, Tanner found a more comfortable position as he waited for the flood to run its course. Although slightly less enthusiastic, the water still rushed down the mountainside, dragging along items picked up on its way through the enemy camp—a chair, a tent, a pair of boots. Then it suddenly slowed, and with an almost audible sigh, the water stopped. Tanner let out a sigh of his own, and his shoulders sagged imperceptibly. Things could have gone a lot worse.

The blowing of the dam and the resulting flood had been a threat hanging over him from the get go. It had been a consideration in all his tactical planning and military strategy, now it was over and done. This could turn out to be a game changer.

\*\*\*\*

Bliss kept pace aloft beside the balloon and her partner Nate. Noodge waited below.

Solace hovered near Tanner as his men scaled the rocks and repelled into the canyon to secure the enemy camp.

With Malachi at her side, Port landed near the destroyed dam. A few yards away, Xandora cringed behind a huge boulder.

Botu lay on the ground, green blood oozing from multiple wounds, the stink rising off of him like an unseen fog. Thurax stood over his body, a bloody knife in his hand.

"He's mine, Portence," Malachi stated, nodding toward the alien mercenary. She straightened, laser pistol at the ready, words of protest on her lips. "We chased one another through time and space. I earned the right," he added.

The warrior in her wanted her own pound of flesh. Bottom line, Thurax was the real reason she ended up on the trash planet. But the pain she had suffered, at least physically, had been swift. Now she realized Malachi had suffered too, in body, heart, and mind— and *not* swiftly at all.

She also understood the male part of him needing

to do it *for her*, to protect her now because he couldn't stop what happened back then.

Malachi drew his own knife, a curved blade used by the Bedouin spice merchants of Askaman. Now in the dead silent atmosphere, Malachi met Thurax. The sound of their exertion was easily detected, and the clashing of metal rang out remarkably loud.

Xandora found the courage to come sneaking out of hiding, and as she edged toward the battling warriors, Port wondered for whom the demi-goddess rooted. One thing for sure, the little spoiled brat-woman wasn't going to interfere.

Port flash moved to stand behind her. "I don't care if you are Mother's pet," she said, jabbing the muzzle of her pistol in Xandora's back. "If you take one more step, I'll laser your ass."

Maybe it was the tone of her voice, or maybe the silly twit finally realized the war was over, but either way she stood still as a statue.

"I knew he was never really mine."

The sadness in Xandora's voice almost squeezed a drop of sympathy out of Port. Almost but not quite. The legendary female had played everyone false. It seemed a fitting retribution for her now to stand alone.

Wringing the flood water from the sleeves of his robe Gorlock stood, in the doorway of the twisted remains of the tractor trailer. He blinked his beady eyes a few times as if in contemplation, perhaps deciding which side he should champion. It seemed obvious who claimed victory. Once Botu had been taken down, the Rep soldiers, not drowned or killed, had surrendered easily, yet Gorlock appeared uncertain.

Glancing back to the main event, she wished

Malachi would go badass-sorcerer on Thurax and be done with it. Right now Malachi was all Fae. He loomed tall, his black battle wings dematerialized as he fought on the ground. A dark specter, his height and agility offset Thurax's size and weight.

With each blow, regardless of who gave or received, Xandora twitched and squealed. She really wasn't cut out to lead an army. Dreams of grandeur, a scheming mind, and the ability to convince the masses to follow her had not been enough. When it came to the nitty-gritty, she couldn't cut it and wanted out.

When the blade on Thurax's knife shattered, Malachi gained the advantage. But the mercenary deflected the next blow with a broken board scooped up off the ground.

Xandora took a step forward. Rather than carrying through with her threat to shoot her, Port grabbed her by the arm. Then she felt the prick of a small blade at her back, just about level with her right kidney.

"Release Xandora, and tell Malachi to lay down his weapon."

She'd been so concerned for Malachi, she hadn't noticed Gorlock circle around behind her. Disarming and overpowering the wimpy necromancer, would be easy enough, but any disturbance might distract Malachi, giving Thurax the edge he needed to kill the man she loved.

She stood frozen in place, the pain increasing along with the pressure of the blade.

"Why don't you lay down *your* weapon instead?"

Lance! At his words, she breathed easier and tightened her grip on Xandora. Glancing over her shoulder she saw the big medical man, in military gear, pointing a Glock at Gorlock's head. Like a superhero, Dr. Lawson had a knack for showing up in the nick of time.

"Thanks partner. How are the wounded doing?"

"The injured at the clinic are all doing well, so I thought I'd pop over to see what's going on here." He lowered the hand gun to waist level, soundly prodding Gorlock when he tried to move sideways.

As two soldiers jogged by, Lance gained their attention. "Secure his hands, gag him, and search him for a wand," he ordered. "We don't need any magical interference," he said, as he waited for the men to incapacitated Gorlock.

Turning back to watch Malachi, it was all she could do not to race forward to stand and fight beside him—like in the old days. It's what she knew, what she thought the future held for them. But fighting went against his sorcerer side, the side that believed in balancing the Multiverse and using power only for the good. Since the last time they'd been together, he seemed to have become more and more attuned to this part of his nature. The future might hold more changes than she anticipated. She was ready for something new if it meant being with him.

Out of breath, Thurax landed fewer and fewer offensive blows with the board he wielded like a baseball bat. Malachi finally kick-boxed the wood from his hands, and landing a stunning blow to Thurax's abdomen, the giant went down like a felled tree.

Malachi stood over him, the coup de grâce would be easy enough to deliver, but she knew Mother had asked Malachi not to kill Thurax. Being unable to return to the realm from whence he came, Mother viewed the warrior-for-hire as being worthy of a modicum of empathy, or some such consideration. It appeared Malachi intended to honor her request.

"On your feet," he ordered, blood dripping from a shoulder wound. Several armed soldiers backed up the request.

Thurax struggled upright. "Kill me, and be done with it. I am ready."

"You're to be taken alive."

"No. I will die like a warrior. You understand what it's like to be confined."

"Thanks to you," Malachi added.

"It will be even worse for me."

Malachi held his ground. Port could only guess at the struggle going on in his mind.

Shoving Malachi aside, Thurax rushed toward Xandora, his hands outstretched as if to strangle her. "It's your fault, you stupid whining female. You got us into this hopeless war."

Port stepped in front of the quaking female, and laser on maximum load, she pulled the trigger. The blast hit Thurax square in his broad chest. Malachi hit him from behind with a bolt of energy. The combined power stopped him in his tracks, his body stiffened, and for a moment he wavered to and fro. A smile overtook the expression of surprise and pain, then he staggered forward and fell at her feet. Laser pistol ready she stared down at him.

"I'm finally home," Thurax said, one arm extended as if reaching for the sky. Then his arm dropped to his side, and he breathed his last.

Xandora took the opportunity to run screaming like a child to the shelter of Hephaestus. Having watched from afar, only now did the old god venture closer. He appeared defeated.

Malachi flash moved to Port's side. "It's over."

She studied his face, not seeing triumph or arrogance in his expression. In the final analysis, taking a life, even Thurax's, hit him hard. This side of him stood as strong as the side that could fight like a demon and keep coming back for more. The love she felt for him in that moment, encompassed her. They were united again, in heart and spirit.

"Yes," she agreed. "*This* is over. But for us, it's just the beginning."

The little half smile, the one that never failed to make her knees weak, teased across his mouth. "A new beginning, indeed. For all of us."

## Chapter Nineteen

Three days had passed since the end of the war. All of Mother's female Fae Warriors, stationed far and wide across the planet, had been successful in bringing the overall conflict to an end. When word spread Xandora had been captured, a complete collapse of enemy forces followed. The Reps surrendered in droves, hoping to be sent back to their home planet.

Now, the evening sun crept toward the mountains as if reluctant to set, and the three Fae Warriors gathered together in the master bedroom of the main house.

Forcing herself to stop fidgeting about the room, Port turned to study her sisters. Bliss, at home in the room she shared with Nate, sat on the big comfy bed combing-out her red hair. Solace stood before the full-length mirror working on her tresses dark as night. For an instant, Port recalled when they were young, sharing a room at the top of the house where they played dress up and wondered what it would be like to make love to a male Fae. It hadn't even occurred to them other male species might be as tempting.

"Mother seemed genuinely sad about Xandora's complete break with this or any reality," Bliss said.

"Let's face it," Solace noted, "Xandora was halfway-to-crazy when she landed on Earth."

"Well, I'm glad she's going to a healing planet."

Leave it to Bliss to show concern for their psychopathic enemy. But her kindness was what made Bliss the beautiful soul she was.

"It's the same place where her sister Pandora resides," Solace reminded, rubbing Saturnalia cream on her bruised thigh, a wound received in the final battle. "If that's not a recipe for disaster, I don't know what is."

"Have to agree with you there." Port continued aimlessly about the room. "And wasn't Mother a sight to see in all her frightful glory dressing down Hephaestus, and warning him to never again get involved in such tomfoolery?"

Solace put the cream away and flopped down into the overstuffed chair in the corner. "Glad I wasn't on the receiving end of that conversation. Old Heph huffed and puffed and headed back to Olympus in record time. He barely had time to pack his droid."

"Serves him right for getting involved in the first place."

Bliss gained her feet, intercepting Port as she wandered by. "Stop pacing so I can do your hair. You've combed it wet, and it's lost all the curl."

Brandishing a comb and brush like domestic weapons, Bliss herded her toward the bed. Port reluctantly sat on the edge "Just don't make me look like the winner of a Medusa contest. And what's with this ceremony anyway?"

"I haven't a clue," Bliss admitted, gently tending her locks. "It's almost as big a mystery as to why your hair turned completely white again, accept for one little patch of blue by your temple. Something is counteracting the damage done by the poison."

"Maybe Malachi wielded some magic," Solace suggested.

"He better not have." Malachi promised not to pull any charms and spells on her again. Even though now she knew back then he'd done it to help her. "Am I the only one who thinks tonight's ritual sounds rather hoity-toity and extravagant for Warrior Women?" she asked, changing the subject.

"Don't knock it," Solace said. "It's fun to be girly for at least a little while. And after we get our new assignments who knows the next time we can party hardy—together."

Those words brought the mood down to ground zero. Port glanced at the three beautiful dresses hanging on hooks along the wall beside the closet door. Except for color, just like the hair of the three sisters, the silky halter dresses were identical in style—fancy but not fussy, and sexy yet classy. What a huge change from the camo fatigues in which they'd been living.

But the entire scenario felt like make-believe, or something surreal. Mother had arranged tonight's event, including the costuming. White for Bliss, the compassionate one—her red hair all the color she needed. Ruby red for Solace, the bold adventurous one—the perfect contrast for her black hair. And for herself—Mother had chosen blue. A dark, dusky blue, like the jewels of the Centaury Mineral planet. Guess Mother knew she could use a hint of color in her life since Malachi had driven the darkness from her soul. The hue would be the perfect backdrop for her white hair.

When a scratching sounded at the door, Port escaped Bliss' handiwork to cross the room to see who might be there. What a surprise to find Mrs. Maxwell. The big feline meowed, and shook her head as if Port could miss the envelope attached with a ribbon around her neck. The missive was addressed to all three sisters. The unblinking stare Mrs. Maxwell drilled into her, screamed she expected compensation for delivery.

"Sorry, girlfriend," Port said, stroking her head, "I haven't any treats on hand." With what sounded like a huff, their furry friend stalked off down the hall, tail in the air. "Don't take it personal," she said, closing the door.

Bliss and Solace hurried to her side, and the three sisters, wearing only their long hair, bikini panties, and curiosity stared down at the note. The envelope felt expensive. The paper within was of equal quality.

*At eighteen hundred hours,*
*Your presence is requested in the dining area.*
*There will be a private on-screen briefing.*
*Don't be late.*

"We better hurry," Solace said, glancing at the clock.

They grabbed the footwear delivered with the dresses. White wedgies with ankle straps and lacey bows for Bliss, black high-heeled ankle boots for Solace, and over-the-knee, fitted boots for Port, the exact color as her dress.

"I hope they have plenty of food at this—whatever it is," Solace said, as they slipped into their respective dresses. "I'm starving."

Port couldn't shake the idea something big was about to happen. And the way Nate, Tanner, and Malachi had been acting, she wouldn't doubt they were in on it. Suddenly she felt more nervous than when they'd faced down Hover Rats and roaring Reptiles.

Before leaving the room, they stood in a circle, the Sisters of Anu. Thinking alike, they all conjured fragile lace wings. They'd been practicing, yet still couldn't maintain them for any significant amount of time. But for the few moments they lasted, this magical memory would link them together even more closely. Laughing, they chanted "The power of three, so shall it be."

****

The Mother board winked on as soon as the three Fae Warriors stood before it in the annex to the dining area. Everyone else seemed suspiciously absent.

"My darling warriors," Mother began. A rare image of her reclining on her fainting couch filled the screen. "You have fought valiantly and victoriously. Now your work here is done. You have also fulfilled your original obligation to me as Fae Warriors. If you so desire, you may continue with future military assignments, or because your home planet remains under my care and auspices, you may accept the alternate assignments I have for you."

Port bristled. It seemed Mother couldn't help trying to run their lives. Of course her species did owe their existence to her. While planning their future, would she be so unkind as to keep her from Malachi—or Bliss from Nate, and Solace from Tanner?

"No third choice?" she dared to ask, desperate to stay with her true love.

Both of her sisters swallowed hard, but stood fast at her side.

"Have some faith, Portence. Although the best laid plans can go awry, from the beginning I have tried to do what I thought best for all of you. And I'm proud of each of you. You are the best of my best, an honor rarely achieved. And it shall be rewarded.

"If you chose not to continue in the military, you must take on trust what will be next for you. It will not be revealed until after tonight's ceremony, and once committed there will be no turning back."

Silence filled the room, heavy and all-encompassing. The sisters reached for one another's hands.

"If it eases your mind," Mother prodded, "Malachi, Nate, and Tanner have already agreed to abide by my ruling."

Holy Carina, of course it eased her mind. Mother sure had a dry sense of humor. She must be bored, or she simply enjoyed toying with them. But the unknown fate caused Port's heart rate to increase. She'd been a warrior most of her long life. It defined her. Of course, it also limited her horizons.

The three sisters studied one another. Were the others just as unsure?

"I'm scared too," Bliss said. "But I think we're all ready to try something new."

Solace nodded, and in unison, they said, "We accept."

Mother smiled, and rose gracefully from her divan like the royalty she was. "Please proceed to the back of the ranch house. We shall begin the ceremony."

****

Assuming the big sister role, Port shepherded her two sisters through the house to the porch. As they stepped down onto the grass, she noted the surrounding trees held tiny lights as if hundreds of fireflies had come to join the party. When a whirring sound filled the air, however, her smile faltered, and she glanced around. Could those blasted Hover Rats have returned for one more shot at them? As the reason for the sound became clear, a collective gasp of surprise escaped all who were gathered in the yard.

It appeared Mother had sent out a call to all Female Fae Warriors within flash-move-flying distance, and now they gathered at Nate's place for one of Mother's spectacular choreographed events. Dressed in silver with wings of gold, they filled the sky, chattering and laughing.

One by one, they touched down, forming two long lines facing one another. They each wore a black wristband in honor of the fallen Fae Warriors.

At the trumpeting of a horn, reminiscent of medieval times, everyone fell silent. Each Fae in the line on the right unfurled a billowy white banner of material, and after handing off one end to the corresponding Fae in the left line, they rose up in the air, hanging motionless, forming a fluttering canopy of white.

"It's a wing-walk," Bliss whispered, eyes wide.

In Fae culture, a wing-walk was similar to a hand-fasting, a commitment of the heart. Not legally binding and either dissolved or renewed in one revolution of their home planet around their sun. The idea of Malachi agreeing to this left Port stunned. It had to be true love for her magic man to not only bind himself to her, but to declare his feelings in such a public display.

A movement to her left caught Port's attention. Malachi stood waiting with Nate and Tanner. Nate stepped forward first. Dressed in his finest black cowboy hat, a string tie, and a Victorian cutaway coat, he took Bliss' hand and they proceeded down the path beneath the fluttering Fae Warrior archway. Faery dust rained down on them, adding a sparkle to Bliss' white dress as Noodge harked and loped along at their side.

Tanner came next to collect Solace. Since the Army E.T. squad had been disbanded, rather than wearing camo, he dressed in his personal uniform of jeans, black T-shirt, and bomber jacket. With Solace's red dress and kicky short boots, they were the perfect match.

Now it was her turn.

Port's Eolh tattoo tingled as Malachi stepped to her side. He wore a black caftan tailored to fit perfectly, especially across his broad chest. Copper rivets gleamed like chain mail along the shoulders and neckline, setting off his amber eyes. His long hair, braided with strips of fabric the same shadowy blue as her dress, declared she belonged to him. Together, they were the color of the sky when dusk overtakes the light to welcome in the night.

Heart pounding in her chest, she took his offered hand and followed the others. At the end of the tunnel of wings sat Mother, her friend Mercury at her back. Lance stood off to her right side, beaming at her like a proud father. He cut quite the dashing figure in his Army blue mess uniform. Alfonso stood off to the left, his girlfriend at his side, Mrs. Maxwell in his arms.

After they'd passed through the wing-walk, the silver-clad Fae Warriors settled back to the ground, maintaining silence as Mother spoke.

"You are now committed to one another for one Fae year, during which time you will carry out the following assignments.

"Bliss and Nate shall remain here on planet Earth to raise and train Raprans. They are rare and much needed in the Multiverse."

Nate let out with a yahoo. Bliss laughed and hugged Noodge. Then she clasped Nate's hand, and smiled up at him.

"Tanner and Solace shall return to the Fae realm. Solace shall train future Fae Warriors in the art of weaponry, and Tanner shall be the first Earth ambassador. The Earth has minerals not present on Kepler 186f, and we have information relative to technological advancements. A worthy exchange toward which to work. "

Solace threw her arms around Tanner's neck and kissed him. He held her tight and spun her around.

"Portence, you shall accompany Malachi back to Mystica where he will complete his training. You will also learn rudimentary magic, and determine how it may apply to Space Counter Intelligence when combined with Fae abilities."

She couldn't have asked for anything more. They would be together on his beautiful home planet. Standing behind her, he wrapped his arms around her. Leaning her head back upon his shoulder, true joy was hers.

"You will have one week here to prepare for your new roles, and to say goodbye to one another."

Being reminded of their impending separation, Port's enthusiasm plummeted.

"Because the three of you were apart for so long, and because your bond is stronger than most, I will allow each of you six pre-authorized time-slips per year to visit one another. This includes passage for your partners as well. So stop looking so sad, and let's party."

Mother slid her hand into Mercury's, and the Fae Warrior guests burst into dancing and singing. Alfonso began setting out a royal feast, and music flowed out of the old Victrola Lance cranked with enthusiasm. Several lovely Fae Warriors gathered around Dr. Lawson. He appeared quite pleased with their attention.

Port wandered off with Malachi. "I couldn't have hoped for more," she said.

He kissed her gently. "Nor I," he agreed. "From now on it's you and me kid…and baby makes three."

Epilogue

If the past week had been the height of frivolity, today screamed dead serious to the max.

Waiting for her sisters, Port stood in Mouse's stall currying the big gray gelding. They were all going for one last ride together. How she would miss the closeness she shared with Bliss and Solace. The three were counterparts of one another. Identical, yet existing in parallel lives, like three parallel universes. And her universe had just been turned on its head.

When Malachi had inferred she was pregnant, passing out had threatened Port for the first time in her life. The truth still had her emotionally off balance. When she'd lost their first child, she had put all thoughts of motherhood aside. She wasn't really the motherly type, at least that's what she'd told herself.

Malachi seemed delighted with the prospect of being a father, and she knew without doubt he would be a really good one. She'd seen the happiness and love in his golden eyes, which made her happy too, but she was the one carrying their progeny. He wouldn't be the one tied down and adventure-less.

She pictured herself huge of belly, trying to lift off the ground with high capacity service wings—and only gaining a mere few inches. She couldn't go gallivanting around the Multiverse trying out new magic-infused fighting techniques when she was as big as a

Gini Rifkin

Mammothon from Epsilon-b. And what about after he or she was born? Talk about terrible twos. The kid would be mostly Fae, but one part mischievous sorcerer, and a whole lot of work.

Lost in thought she stopped brushing the dappled neck until Mouse nickered and gently nosed her. She was going to miss this big gray gelding. She'd use her last magic wish if she thought taking him with her was the right thing to do. But that would be selfish. Mouse had been raised with Rocket and Raven, and he'd be lost without them. Bliss promised to take good care of him. He'd be okay.

Brushing away, she tried picturing herself, Malachi, and the baby as a happy family trooping through the woods at the Summer Solstice. This image brought a smile. Already she felt a connection to the babe, and she'd roar and fight like a mother Yukla bear to protect him—him! Guess it was a boy. But she felt helpless to control her own future, and her body. Just look what happened to her hair. The poison had left it streaked with blue. Had the purity of the new life within her changed it back?

Chattering and laughing, her sisters entered the barn, Noodge bounding along behind them.

"Hey, about time you guys showed up." She tried not showing her concern in front of them, but she was scared.

"Being a mother will be the best adventure of all," Bliss said, reading her mind. Her redheaded sister bounced up and down on her toes, and Solace danced down the aisle in the center of the barn.

They'd been this way ever since she'd told them she was pregnant.

"Oh Port, we promise to be the best Aunties in Fae history, and that's a long, long time. Solace even promised to learn to knit, and I'll train Noodge to babysit when you come to visit."

When she came to visit? The reality of their separation cut deep, making her panic all the more. Giving Mouse a hug, she left the stall and locked the half/gate.

Solace grabbed a banana Popsicle from the mini-fridge in the tack room and brought it to her. They knew she craved the cool treat now more than ever. What she really wanted was a big pitcher of margaritas, but she supposed it wouldn't be good for the little Halfling. Already he was dictating her life.

"Now, for sure, you'll have to go back up on Spacebook," Solace said.

"Oh yes. We'll need at least weekly updates and pictures." Bliss agreed.

Yikes. This was freaking her out all the more. They knew she didn't like Spacebook. It was such a time suck. At least she'd have thirteen months to get used to the idea before the babe appeared. It was just all too much to take in.

Finished with the popsicle, she tucked the stick in her pocket, and reaching out toward her sisters, she gathered them near. Regardless of where they were or what services they performed for Mother, they would always be warriors, and they would always be sisters. Joining hands, they formed a circle, slowly walking around and around. Coming to a halt, they tightened the formation, raising joined hands in the middle, and right then she knew all would be well.

"Here's to the Sisters of Anu," Bliss called out.

Noodge gave an honest to goodness howl, and ran around the barn. The sisters took a step back and repeated in unison—

*Seasons come, seasons go.*
*Together in spirit, so shall we grow.*
*If need arise, and one should call,*
*Two will respond, and give their all.*
*Sisters mine from before our birth,*
*Sharing our lives in sadness and mirth.*
*We stand united, for all to see.*
*The power of three, so shall it be.*

# Fae Warriors' Glossary of Terms and Places

ATLATL: Used to increase the leverage in throwing a spear. It is the first compound weapon.

ANIME: Japanese Adventure Cartoons.

AQUEOUS II: A training planet, mostly water.

CAMORAE: A planet in the Redshift 7 galaxy.

CHAMELEON DNA: mixed with other animals' DNA allows them to change color at will.

CARONIUM: Planet where the purest gold in the Multiverse is mined.

CARPATHENA: Planet of the yogi masters.

CETI 9: Home of the Manshees.

CRONOS 12: Where the male Fae Warriors are fighting Outworlders.

CRYSTAL COSMOS NO. 5: Solace's favorite perfume.

CRYSTALLINE B: The ice planet where crystals are mined in the frost fields.

DARRIUS III: Planet of the salt fields.

DARRIUS V: Trash planet of the Crap-eater Megaderms.

EPSILON-B: Planet of ice caves.

EXOSPHERE: The outermost region of the earth's atmosphere.

KEPLER 186F: the Fae Warriors' home planet

LIGHT-YEARS: The distance light travels in one year. (Nearly 6 trillion miles).

MERCURY: Mother's messenger "boy" and lover.

METROSEXUAL: Metropolitan heterosexual.

MILESIANS: The ancestors of the modern Irish.

MMA: Mixed martial arts.

MYSTICA: The planet of illusion.

NANOSECOND: One billionth of a second.

NORSE-GUARD 12: One of fifty fabricated planets ringing the edge of our universe.

OUT-WORLDERS: Those beyond the home galaxy.

PARADISE III: A recreational planet.

PARSEC: 3.26 light years.

PRION: Imperfect protein, causing conditions such as mad cow disease.

PROXIGEAN SPRING TIDE: An extremely high tide, very unusual.

RAPRAN: Companion animal, looks half mastiff and half Bengal tiger, with a touch of kangaroo.

REMEDIUM 5: A healing planet.

RIGEL 5: The prison planet.

SATURNALIA CREAM: Made on the home planet for soothing bruises and wounds.

SCI: Space Counter Intelligence.

SYZYGY TIDE: When the earth, moon, and sun are aligned.

TERAHEATHAN PLANET: Known for art and spun glass.

THE DRAGON LORDS OF ANU: The offspring of the fallen angels (Anunnaki).

THE SISTERS OF ANU: Bliss' super hero name for the three sisters.

THE ABSOLUTE ZONE or A ZONE: the area between universes. No man's land.

TROOPING: Fae traveling the woodlands in joyous groups, especially on Equinoxes and Solstices.

TUATHA DE DANANN: The people of the goddess, ancestors to the Fae.

## A word about the author...

Gini Rifkin writes adventurous romance—past, present, and into the future—sometimes with a bit of magic or fantasy, but always with a happy ending.

When not reading or writing, she greatly enjoys caring for a menagerie of abandoned farm animals on her little patch of land in Colorado. Her writing keeps her hungry to learn new things, and she considers family and friends her most treasured of gifts.

~

## Other titles from Gini Rifkin
## Available from The Wild Rose Press, Inc.

*The Dragon And The Rose*
*Lady Gallant*
*Iron Heart*
*Special Delivery*
*Victorian Dream*
*A Cowboy's Fate*
*The Fae Warrior Series:*
*Solace*
*Bliss*

Thank you for purchasing
this publication of The Wild Rose Press, Inc.

If you enjoyed the story, we would appreciate your
letting others know by leaving a review.

For other wonderful stories,
please visit our on-line bookstore at
www.thewildrosepress.com.

For questions or more information
contact us at
info@thewildrosepress.com.

The Wild Rose Press, Inc.
www.thewildrosepress.com

Stay current with The Wild Rose Press, Inc.

Like us on Facebook

https://www.facebook.com/TheWildRosePress

And Follow us on Twitter
https://twitter.com/WildRosePress

www.ingramcontent.com/pod-product-compliance
Lightning Source LLC
Chambersburg PA
CBHW060926180626
46817CB00004B/1420